From Megan Maitland's Diary

Dear Diary,

Ellie just walked in on me a few minutes ago and laughed because a woman my age would still be writing in a diary like a teenager. But I must admit there are times when I do feel like a teenager, with things around me whirling out of control. So much to do, so much to keep track of. Especially now that William is gone. Three years and I still miss him.

Despite the ups and downs, the demands on my time, it's been such a wonderful life so far. William was so good to me, helping me turn this dream of mine into a reality. It's hard to believe that Maitland Maternity is almost twenty-five years old now, but I'm just about to hold a press conference to announce the gala anniversary party. Pretty good for a poor girl who was once lost and pregnant herself. R.J. just knocked on my door, so I'd better end here. It's "show time"!

Megan

Dear Reader,

There's never a dull moment at Maitland Maternity! This unique and now world-renowned clinic was founded twenty-five years ago by Megan Maitland, widow of William Maitland, of the prominent Austin, Texas, Maitlands. Megan is also matriarch of an impressive family of seven children, many of whom are active participants in the everyday miracles that bring children into the world.

As our series begins, the family is stunned by the unexpected arrival of an unidentified baby at the clinic—unidentified, except for the claim that the child is a Maitland. Who are the parents of this child? Is the claim legitimate? Will the media's tenacious grip on this news damage the clinic's reputation? Suddenly, rumors and counterclaims abound. Women claiming to be the child's mother materialize out of the woodwork! How will Megan get at the truth? And how will the media circus affect the lives and loves of the Maitland children—Abby, the head of gynecology, Ellie, the hospital administrator, her twin sister, Beth, who runs the day care center, Mitchell, the fertility specialist, R.J., the vice president of operations—even Anna, who has nothing to do with the clinic, and Jake, the black sheep of the family?

Please join us each month over the next year as the mystery of the Maitland baby unravels, bit by enticing bit, and book by captivating book!

Marsha Zinberg
Senior Editor and Editorial Co-ordinator, Special Projects

MARIE FERRARELLA

Dad by Choice

Silhouette Books

Published by Silhouette Books
America's Publisher of Contemporary Romance

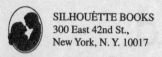

SILHOUÉTTE BOOKS
300 East 42nd St.,
New York, N.Y. 10017

ISBN 0-373-65062-0

DAD BY CHOICE

Copyright © 2000 by Harlequin Books S.A.

Marie Ferrarella is acknowledged as the author of this work.

Visit Silhouette at www.eHarlequin.com

Printed in U.S.A.

Prolific romance author Marie Ferrarella claims, "I was born writing, which must have made the delivery especially difficult for my mother!" Born in West Germany of Polish parents, she came to America when she was four years of age. For an entire year, Marie and her family explored the eastern half of the country before finally settling in New York. It was there, at the age of fourteen, that she met the man she would marry, her first true love, Charles Ferrarella.

During her days at Queens College, acting started to lose its glamour as Marie spent more and more time writing. After receiving her English degree, specializing in Shakespearean comedy, Marie and her family moved to Southern California, where she still resides today. After an interminable seven weeks apart, Charles decided he couldn't live without her, and came out to California to marry his childhood sweetheart. Marie, who has written over one hundred novels, has one goal: to entertain, to make people laugh and feel good. "That, and a really good romantic evening with my husband." She keeps her fingers crossed that her many fans enjoy reading her books as much as she enjoys writing them.

To Leslie Wainger, my patron saint of all good things.

PROLOGUE

THE SOUND OF HER OWN heavy breathing filled her head. Her heart was racing so hard, it felt as if it were on the verge of vibrating out of her chest.

At the end of the alley she stopped running.

As her breathing steadied, she felt a satisfied smile begin to form on her lips, twisting them upward, until anyone seeing her would have ventured to say she looked positively jubilant.

And downright wicked.

But there was no one to see her. Luck had been with her when her patience and her temper had both snapped.

Luck, so much a part of the world she had originally come from, had not been more than a fleeting visitor. Nice to know it was on her side for a change.

A sense of triumph began to take hold. There'd been no one to witness what she had done to claim what was so rightfully hers.

Not hers by any standards passed down through the courts with its legal mumbo jumbo, but that didn't really matter. It was hers nonetheless. She deserved it. Had earned it. Earned it through all those months of careful planning and plotting. Of empty smiles and emptier promises, of befriending people she secretly hated. And now, finally, it was almost hers.

So close, so close.

Sucking in a huge gulp of air to banish the last of

the tiny white pinpricks of light dancing before her eyes, Janelle Maitland Jones hurried back to where the key to her future had been left unprotected on the steps of Maitland Maternity Clinic.

Her smile deepened, but never reached her eyes. Maitland Maternity. How fitting. How damn, ironically fitting.

She almost laughed out loud.

Suddenly, the sound of voices began to mix with the faint buzzing in her head. Raised voices, laced with excitement, all talking at once. Janelle glanced over her shoulder down the alley.

Had someone seen her drag that insufferable bitch's body back there, after all? Had they seen what she'd done?

But the voices weren't coming from the alley. They were coming from the direction of the clinic.

Janelle froze in her tracks, horror spilling over her like black tar, smothering her smugness.

Reporters and camera crews had materialized from nowhere, swarming around the back entrance to the clinic. Blocking her view. Blocking off more than her path.

Biting off a vicious curse, she faded into a doorway at the edge of the alley as frustration threatened to overpower her. Caught halfway between heaven and hell, she was completely cut off from her triumph.

Cut off from the money.

So far, so far…

CHAPTER ONE

DR. ABBY MAITLAND was doing her best not to look as impatient as she felt.

Just down the hall in Maitland Maternity Clinic, patients sat in her waiting room on tasteful, blue-cushioned chairs, chosen to afford optimum comfort to women who were for the most part in an uncomfortable condition. She was booked solid without so much as a ten-minute window of breathing space. She'd come into the clinic running slightly behind and praying that no one would see fit to go into labor this morning.

That was when her mother had waylaid her.

Abby had always had difficulty saying no to her mother, not out of a sense of obligation but one of pure affection. It was hard to say no to a woman who had gone out of her way all her life to make sure that her children were happy and well cared for. Today was no different.

Abby supposed that the request to stand by her mother's side as Megan Kelly Maitland met the press this morning shouldn't have come as a surprise. Abby had been born into this a goldfish-bowl existence, where almost every detail of her life, and of her family's, was periodically dissected for newsworthiness. Especially if the media was having a slow week.

These days, with tabloid journalism running rampant on almost every cable channel and lurid headlines leaping out from every supermarket checkout counter, "newsworthy" was usually synonymous with scandalous.

But not in their case, thank God. The Maitlands, with their penchant for charitable donations and the clinic her mother and late father had cofounded all those years ago, were the press's vanilla ice cream. Comforting, ever-present—but uneventful. The closest they had to a ribbon of contrasting chocolate was her younger brother, Jake, with his mysterious comings and goings and secret life-style.

Lucky Jake, Abby thought as she followed her mother and two of her siblings to the rear entrance. He wasn't here to go through this with them.

But wealth, Abby knew, brought certain obligations, and she was far too much her mother's daughter to turn her back on that. Although there were days when she would have loved to be given the opportunity, just to see what it felt like.

Today, for one.

Abby glanced at her watch for the third time in as many minutes. With a bit of luck, this wouldn't take too long. She absolutely hated being late.

"I don't see why you need all of us, Mother," she heard herself murmuring, despite her good intentions.

Megan Maitland smiled as she gently pushed back a strand of Abby's dark hair that had fallen wantonly into her eyes. The same lock she had been pushing back ever since Abby had had enough hair on her head to run a brush through. A wave of nostalgia whispered through Megan. Her children had gotten so big, so independent.

Her sharp, dark blue eyes swept over her son R.J. and daughter Ellie standing beside her. R.J. was the oldest of the seven, and Ellie and her twin, Beth, were the youngest, with Abby in the middle. Megan wished all her children could be here today when she made the announcement. It was just a silly little press conference, she knew, and they had all promised to come to the party that was being given in honor of the clinic once the plans were finalized. But she missed her children when they weren't around. Missed the sound of their laughter, their voices.

She was as proud of them as she could be, but there were times when she longed for the old days, when they were young and she could keep them all within the reach of an embrace.

Megan blinked, silently forbidding a tear to emerge. She was becoming a foolish old woman before her time. What would William say if he could have seen her? He would have teased her out of it, she knew, while secretly agreeing with her.

She missed him most of all.

Her smile, soft and gentle, widened as she answered Abby's question. "For moral support, darling. I need you for moral support."

R.J. shrugged. Megan knew this was eating into his precious time as president of Maitland Maternity Clinic, but he would never say no to her. Her love for him had been reciprocated from the day she and William had adopted him and his younger sister Anna after their father had deserted them. Although rightfully they could have called her Aunt Megan, she had never felt anything but maternal love for William's niece and nephew.

"Don't see why moral support should have to enter into it, Mother," R.J. muttered, looking more somber than usual. "We're just announcing that there's going to be a party celebrating the clinic's twenty-fifth anniversary. Not much moral support required for that."

A tinge of pity stirred within Megan. R.J. didn't smile nearly enough. In this last year he seemed to have become even more work-oriented than ever.

Ellie, her youngest, whom Megan had appointed hospital administrator despite her tender age of twenty-five, grinned at her serious oldest brother.

"Oh, I don't know," she cheerfully disagreed. "I think facing the press requires a great deal of moral support." She exchanged glances with Abby, a bit of her childhood adoration for her older sister still evident. "I always get the feeling they're waiting for something juicy to bite into."

"That's because they are." Abby could see the trucks from the various cable channels in and around Austin, Texas, through the window that faced the rear of the clinic. "Though I am surprised that so many of them have turned out. After all, this is just a human-interest story to be buried on page twelve."

R.J. tucked his tie neatly beneath his vest. A glint of humor crossed his lips. "Page twelve? If I have to stand on the back steps of the clinic and grin at those hyenas, it better get us lines on at least page four."

Abby patted his arm affectionately. "Don't grin too hard, R.J. Your face might crack."

Though Abby had always known that R.J. and Anna were really her cousins, there had never been a dividing line between any of the Maitland children. They had all been raised with the same amount of affection, shouldering the same amount of responsibility and parental expectation. As a sister, Abby loved R.J., and as a doctor she worried about him at times.

He pretended to shrug off her arm. "Let's get this over with."

Abby cocked her head. The noise outside the back

doors had grown from a dull din to something of a roar. "Is it my imagination, or are the natives getting more restless?"

Ellie frowned. "They do sound louder than usual." She looked at her older sister with a silent question.

Abby in turn glanced at her mother. Whatever it was, they'd find out soon enough. "Ready?"

The tall, regal woman beside Abby squared her shoulders. Wearing a navy-blue suit with white trim at the collar and cuffs, her soft white hair drawn into a French twist, Megan Maitland looked more like their older sister than a woman in her sixty-second year.

"As I'll ever be," Megan acknowledged.

"Then let's get this show on the road," Abby declared.

R.J. pushed open the doors before Abby had a chance to do so. But instead of the forward thrust of raised mikes, invasive cameras and intrusive reporters, they found themselves staring at the backs of heads. To a person, the reporters and camera crews were focusing their attention on something off to the side of the clinic's rear entrance.

Abby glanced at her brother, who seemed as much in the dark as any of them. "What the—?"

She edged forward. Had someone decided to stage a publicity stunt and dramatically go into labor on the clinic's back steps instead of coming inside? Maitland Maternity, established by her parents so that no woman would be forced to have her child without medical help, had somehow turned into the darling of the rich and famous as well as that of the emotionally and financially needy. And among those celebrities were some who had what Abby could only term as a bizarre sense of humor.

Because it wasn't in her nature to hang back where

either her family or her professional life was concerned, Abby didn't wait for her brother to take charge. Instead, she pushed her way farther through the tight throng, determined to find out what had so firmly captured the media's attention.

The next moment, Abby knew. And it was all she could do to keep her mouth from dropping open.

There was a baby on the back steps. A baby, covered with a blanket and lying in a wicker basket. Looking closer, she saw that there was actually a piece of paper pinned to the blanket.

Abby looked around, half expecting someone to come forward and announce that this was all a stunt of some sort. Or a thoughtless prank. It had to be one or the other. This was where women came to have their babies, not leave them.

From where she stood, Megan was unable to see for herself what all the commotion was about. "Abby, what's going on?"

"It's a baby." Abby tossed the words over her shoulder to her mother.

It was as if the sound of her voice were the flag coming down at the starting gate at the Indianapolis 500. The single sentence unleashed a deafening roar as all the reporters hurled their questions toward her at once.

Abby recognized Chelsea Markum, the fast-rising reporter of *Tattle Today TV,* a new explore-all news program. The woman was obviously determined to reach the top of her profession and stay there. That meant being first whenever humanly possible.

Pushing her microphone into her cameraman's hand, she elbowed another reporter out of the way and reached for the baby. Slipping her hands within the basket, she triumphantly picked the baby up.

The mewling sound the infant made was all but swallowed up by the noise surrounding them. But Abby could hear it. It shot straight through to her heart and galvanized her. Her eyes narrowed as she pushed her way closer.

"And there's a note," Chelsea declared to the crowd, ripping it from the blanket.

"What's it say?" someone behind her demanded.

Excitedly, Chelsea read, "'Dear Megan Maitland. This baby is a Maitland. Please take care of him until I can again.'"

Armed with anger and indignation, Abby physically pushed a cameraman aside to reach the innocent infant, who had been turned into a sideshow attraction.

Without a single word, she took the baby from the reporter and turned away.

Like a hailstorm, questions continued to fly at her from all sides—fast, furious and callous. Abby gave no indication that she heard any of them. All she wanted to do was reach the back doors and walk through them.

Suddenly, R.J. was on one side of her and Ellie on the other, buffering her from the crowd and allowing her to retreat with the baby in her arms. Abby's stony expression dissolved and she smiled her relief. She saw R.J. hang back a second to pick up the basket. He looked decidedly paler to her than he had when they had walked outside.

He saw it, too, she thought. The ghostly whisper of a scandal had finally found its way to the Maitland door.

Armed with her reclaimed microphone, Chelsea shoved it into R.J.'s face. "Is the baby yours?" she demanded.

Abby bit back the urge to tell the woman what she could do with her question and where she could next put her microphone.

"Whose is it?" The question echoed over and over again from all sides. "Which one of the Maitlands is the father?"

A tall, redheaded man with a trace of mustard on his shirt front pushed a mike at Megan. "C'mon, Mrs. Maitland, we've all got a living to make. Which of your sons is responsible for this baby?"

Megan Maitland lifted her chin regally and faced the crowd that had been, only minutes earlier, awaiting her arrival with polite smiles and banal good wishes.

"None of them, to the best of my knowledge."

Queen Victoria couldn't have defended the realm better, Abby thought, making eye contact with her mother. But she knew the answer wouldn't satisfy anyone.

"...Who are you covering for?"

"...Hey, give us a break. We're not all well-off like you."

"...You might as well come clean now. It'll all come out eventually."

Megan looked sharply in the direction the last question had come from, but she focused on no one, talking to the crowd in general.

"The truth usually does, if we're lucky," she agreed. "This press conference is at an end."

Turning on her heel, Megan waved Abby and Ellie in before her, then followed, leaving R.J. to cover the retreat.

He did, then ushered the women into his office quickly. Caught off guard, his secretary looked startled as they entered. She raised a quizzical eyebrow at Abby before turning toward R.J.

"Don't let anyone in, Dana," he ordered. Dana began to open her mouth. "And I mean *anyone*." With that, he closed the door to his inner office. Only then did he turn to the others. Avoiding the infant, he looked directly at his mother. "Is this someone's idea of a joke?"

There was sweat on his brow, Abby realized. Her glance went from the baby to R.J. But the baby was hardly more than an infant, perhaps a month or so old, and no outstanding feature seemed to link them.

Nothing but the slight nervousness her brother was attempting to hide.

Abby dismissed the thought, annoyed with herself that she'd allowed the media circus outside to get to her and dignify the unthinkable with even a silent question. The baby couldn't be his. He would have admitted it long before now, if it were. R.J. was far too upstanding to shirk his responsibilities. That was one of the reasons he was so perfect to head up the clinic.

But he was human, for all that, a small voice whispered in her head, and humans had weaknesses.

There had to be another explanation. Besides, he wasn't the only brother she had, she reminded herself. R.J.'s pale color was probably due to nothing more than the shock of a scandal finally touching the family.

"A dribble glass is a joke," Megan replied quietly, struggling to make sense of the situation. The infant suddenly voiced his displeasure, and her eyes, as well as her heart, were drawn to him. "A baby isn't a joke."

Megan experienced the maternal pull she always felt at the sight of a baby. Forgetting for a moment the note, the accusations and the implications that went along with them, she took the infant from her daughter.

A soft warmth pervaded her chest, then flooded

through her. She smiled down at the small, scrunched-up face. "Hello, little stranger. Where's your mommy?"

Holding the child, feeling the small life wriggle against her breast took her back. Back to the times she'd given birth. To the first time she'd held each of her children in her arms.

No, she reminded herself, not each. Not the first one. She hadn't been allowed to hold that baby. Her father had had the stillborn infant whisked away before she could even see him. Or touch him.

He'd done it for her own good, he had said. To save her heartache. To help her to move on. She had been seventeen at the time, and there had been so much more of life ahead of her. He'd been afraid she'd cling to the memory of a dead baby if she'd held it to her.

But there were times, even now, so very many years later, that Megan wished she'd had just that one opportunity to make a bond. And say goodbye.

She realized that her children were looking at her, concern in their eyes. Waiting.

Forcing a smile to her lips, she returned the infant to Abby. "Take him to Ford and have him checked out. I want to be sure that this baby is all right."

"And then?" Ellie asked.

Megan pressed her lips together as she passed her hand over the tiny head. She looked down at the infant. And noticed a small bracelet encircling the child's flailing wrist. "And then we'll see."

"Ellie's just uptight because he doesn't have any insurance cards for her to photocopy." Abby was being deliberately flippant, hoping to distract her mother.

Ellie caught on quickly. "Careful, before I photocopy you," she countered.

Though he kept to himself a good deal, this time R.J. was on the same wavelength as his sisters. "You can't photocopy something that doesn't leave a shadow," he interjected.

Megan knew why they were doing this, why they were bantering carelessly at a time when they should have been shoring up their defenses. To distract her. Even though she had fought so many battles on her own, even though she had managed to rise above her poor beginnings and the tragedy that haunted her to become the respected matriarch of a wealthy socially prominent family, her children still felt they had to protect her.

And she loved them for it. And for countless other reasons. If this baby did turn out to be a Maitland, her feelings wouldn't change. There would just be one more child to love.

With affection, she terminated the banter. "We'll discuss the abilities of the copy machine and your sister's lack of shadow later. Abby, go." Shooing her off, Megan turned to the remaining duo in the spacious office. She wanted to adjourn to her own office, where she had faced her toughest decisions, had had her finest triumphs. She felt secure there. "R.J., Ellie, come."

Abby raised a brow and glanced toward her sister. "Ever notice how she treats the kids like dogs?"

"Go," Megan repeated.

Abby hurried off.

"WHAT'S GOING ON?" Dana's question met Abby the moment she walked out of R.J.'s office.

"I'm not really sure," Abby confessed. Dana Dillinger was one of her closest friends and she didn't feel right about brushing her off, but she was *really* running behind now. "Get R.J. to tell you."

Dana shook her head and sighed. "As if R.J. could ever share anything but reports and schedules with me."

Abby raced out the door and hurried to the elevator banks, nodding at several people she knew. Mercifully, the elevator was empty. She got in and quickly pressed the button. Only once the doors had slid closed again did she glance at the baby in her arms.

The eyes were blue, as were those of most infants, and opened wide, as if he were drinking in the entire world around him and storing it up for future reference. Abby felt a tug in her heart, the way she did with each child she held in her arms.

"So, am I really your aunt Abby, or is this just some kind of a hoax?" In response, the baby squirmed. "No offense, little guy, but I really hope it's a hoax. Not that I wouldn't mind having you in the family, you understand, but…"

The squirming was followed by a gurgling sound a moment before the infant turned an extreme shade of beet red. A second later, a distinct odor began to rise from the vicinity of his tiny bottom.

How could anything so small smell so bad? she wondered.

"Okay, be that way," Abby murmured, shifting the baby. This was going to mean a little extra work for Katie, she thought. As if the pediatric nurse didn't already have enough to do…

DROPPING THE CHART Ford had just given her into the To Be Filed pile, already four deep at nine-thirty in the morning, pediatric nurse Katie Topper turned when she heard the private entrance door opening. She flashed a quick smile when she saw who it was. Then a small furrow formed between her brows when she noticed the baby.

"Abby, what's up?"

Like Dana, Katie was one of Abby's closest friends. But if she'd had no time to fill Dana in, she had even less time now. Her mother's unintentional ambush had cost her more than half an hour. The way her luck was running, she'd probably be called away for a multiple birth on her way back down.

"Got a new patient for Ford to check out." Abby glanced toward the reception area. There were only three patients waiting their turn with the pediatric surgeon. "Mother's orders."

Katie glanced behind Abby, expecting to see another woman entering. "Where is the baby's mother?"

An involuntary sigh escaped her lips. Abby looked at the infant. "That's the 64,000-dollar question."

"But you just said—" Katie began.

"My mother," Abby clarified. "She wants Ford to check him out as soon as possible."

The request was unusual. "What's wrong with him?" Katie sniffed the air. "Other than the obvious. Did you have to bring me a ripe one?"

"Sorry." Abby laughed. "And to answer your other question—nothing, I hope."

"Curiouser and curiouser," Katie said. She reached for an empty folder. "So, what name do I put on the chart?"

"This—" Abby held the infant up "—is Baby X."

Katie put down her pen and looked at Abby. "Is this some kind of a joke?"

R.J.'s words, Abby thought. "I wish. Someone just dropped him off on our doorstep. Classic note pinned to the blanket and everything. All that was missing was snow and a heart-wrenching musical score.'' She shook her head. It wasn't the baby's fault, but that didn't change anything. ''The press is going to have a field day.''

Katie took the baby from her. ''The press?''

Abby nodded. ''They were there for Mother's announcement about the clinic's twenty-fifth anniversary celebration. They liked this story better.'' She glanced toward the door leading to the first examining room. It was closed. ''Tell Ford I'll be by as soon as I can manage.''

Katie shifted the baby to her other arm. The outer door buzzed softly, announcing another patient. ''What do we do with Baby X until then?''

Abby paused in the doorway, one hand on the knob. ''See if you can get him to talk.'' With that, she hurried away.

THE DARKNESS ABOUT HER lifted slowly, like a heavy curtain being drawn away. A dull, persistent ache came to fill its place, and it felt as if there was something inching down her forehead just above her brow.

With fingers that didn't quite feel as if they belonged to her, she touched the spot on her head. A stickiness registered. She looked at her fingers.

Blood.

Her blood.

Why?

She gazed around slowly. The ache wouldn't allow her to move quickly. She was on the ground, in an alley of some sort, and it was daylight.

Relying on shaky limbs, she managed to rise to her

feet. As she did so, she became aware of another sensation.

Her arms felt empty. As if she had been holding something that was gone now.

But what?

Dazed, confused, she looked down at them, trying to remember what it was she'd lost.

Trying to remember anything at all.

But there was nothing but a huge void.

She couldn't remember.

Anything.

A noise caught her attention. Like a magnet of hope, it drew her around.

There was a man standing at the end of the alley. A man dressed in blue. A policeman.

He looked at her uncertainly, stepping forward. "Can I help you, ma'am?"

A sob caught in her throat as she made her way toward him. "Yes."

Suddenly the world began to shimmer. Spinning, it retreated from her until there was nothing left but a tiny opening for the light to squeeze through. And then, even that was gone.

Boneless, she fell to the ground.

CHAPTER TWO

KYLE MCDERMOTT SHIFTED in his chair. He'd lost count of how many times now. Had he been wearing the jeans he so rarely put on these days, he would have rested his ankle across his thigh. But that wouldn't fit, given the three-piece suit he was wearing. Besides, it would somehow seem disrespectful to the other occupants of the room, most of whom looked as if they hadn't been truly comfortable in months.

He glanced at his sister. He knew that Marcie had been uncomfortable for a while now. She was the reason he was here, suffering and growing progressively more agitated.

Kyle didn't like waiting, had never been able to tolerate it. And even if he could have, he wouldn't have liked waiting here, in a room full of women whose bodies were in various stages of pending motherhood. He felt out of place, the lone male in the midst of some secret female sorority he had no right to be invading.

As far back as he could remember, Kyle McDermott had never thought of himself as an actual people person. His talents lay in other directions. It was only because he loved his baby sister, Marcie, that he was here. And paying dearly for it.

Trying vainly to stifle an exasperated sigh that begged to be exhaled, he glanced at his watch. Forty-seven minutes. Forty-seven minutes past the scheduled time for Marcie's appointment.

Where the hell is that doctor?

Never raising her eyes from the magazine she was flipping through, Marcie leaned over in his direction. "It's not going to go any faster if you keep looking at it."

"I don't want it to go faster. I just want your doctor to get here."

He was trying to keep his voice down, but it seemed as if every set of eyes had turned in his direction. He should never have let Marcie talk him into coming along. It was bad enough having to be her coach, without enduring this.

"When I told you to get your doctor's first morning appointment, I didn't think he started at noon."

"She." The word left her lips tersely. Marcie gave up the pretense of reading and closed the magazine. "Can't you even remember that? I must have told you a hundred times."

"A dozen," he corrected out of habit, remembering now. Of course, he knew Maitland was a woman. It had just slipped his mind, that's all. He saw Marcie's brows draw together the way they always did when she stubbornly dug in. He didn't want another argument. This was neither the time nor the place. For the sake of peace, he tried for a truce. "Sorry, Marce, I'm preoccupied."

"You're *always* preoccupied."

It wasn't the first time Marcie had flung the accusation at him. And to a certain extent, it was true. His mind was always going off in a dozen different directions, taken up by a myriad of details. Maybe that was why she'd turned to Billy Madison in the first place.

This bickering wasn't going to get them anywhere, Kyle thought. And the only thing worse than sitting here in the middle of a room full of pregnant women was arguing with his sister in a room full of pregnant women. He shouldn't have come today. If it really meant that much to Marcie to have him along on an office visit, next week would be better for him.

Fed up and tired, Kyle began to rise. Marcie's hurt look came as no surprise. He fielded it. "Listen, I'd better go. I'll leave the car for you and I'll call a cab."

Marcie reached out to catch his arm, then stopped herself. "Afraid you'll miss your precious meeting?"

If they hadn't already been at the center of everyone's attention, they were now. He'd raised her better than this, Kyle thought. But then, he reminded himself, if he'd truly raised her well, she wouldn't be in this condition.

Kyle gave up trying to be discreet, though for the moment, he sank back down in his chair. "At this rate, I'm afraid I'll miss the rest of my life. Your doctor doesn't seem to respect the fact that other people have schedules, too."

Having said nothing out of the ordinary and certainly nothing that wasn't true, he saw no reason for Marcie's suddenly wide eyes.

Until he heard the voice behind him.

"Oh, but I do, Mr. McDermott. It is Mr. McDermott, isn't it? I'm assuming that since you're lecturing Marcie and you definitely look older than eighteen, you have to be the big brother she's been telling me about, and not Billy."

It wasn't often that Kyle could be accused of being caught off guard. Since his father's death more than ten years ago, when he'd suddenly found himself sole guardian of his younger sister, he'd tried to be prepared for all contingencies way ahead of time. But the woman's voice, amused, low and reminiscent of aged bourbon taken slow on a long winter's evening, did just that.

And the sight of her did even more.

Having expected to see a dour, matronly looking woman in sensible black shoes, an austere hairdo and utilitarian clothing, he was momentarily rendered speechless by the slender brunette in three-inch heels and a fashionable, light blue suit that looked as if it had been made for her.

The blue brought out her eyes.

He had no idea why he thought that, or even noticed. He wasn't given to details like that. Not about people, only about microchips and semiconductors, like the one he'd perfected—the one that was responsible for his fortune.

Well, Abby thought, it seemed as if good looks ran in the family. Marcie McDermott had struck her as a beauty the first moment she'd met the poised teenager. On her brother, Kyle, those dark good looks were even more arresting, although on him they seemed to come with a certain edginess.

That could have been due to the frown on his lips.

Gamely, Abby put out her hand, feeling just a tad like someone bearding a lion in its den.

"Hi, I'm Abby Maitland, Marcie's doctor, and I'm sorry about the delay." She looked around the waiting room. It was more packed than she'd expected. Some of her patients had turned up early for their appointments. Murphy's Law. "Ladies, I'll see you all in due time. I'm afraid I was unavoidably detained, but I'll try to make up for it." Crossing to the inner area, she nodded a greeting at her nurse. "Lisa, please show Marcie into room 1. I'll be there in three minutes. Faster, if the buttons on the lab coat don't give me a hard time."

The nurse she'd addressed as Lisa, a willowy blonde, came to the doorway, a chart in her hands. "Looks like you're up, Marcie." But when Kyle rose to accompany his sister, Lisa stopped him with a slight shake of her head. "Not yet, Mr. McDermott. I'll come get you when we're ready."

Great, Kyle thought. More waiting. Now he really couldn't leave. He didn't want Marcie to come out and find him gone. God knows what she'd think or do then. For the most part, she'd always been a levelheaded kid, he thought, but this pregnancy had thrown her off.

As it had him. With effort, he banked down the resentment that rose within him.

Kyle sank back onto the seat, resigned. How had he gotten to this place in his life? he wondered. Wasn't this where the good part was supposed to come in? He'd struggled hard these last fifteen years to get through college and make a go of his business, at times financing things on a shoestring that seemed as if it would snap at any second. He'd made sacrifices to keep the company going, a great many sacrifices. He knew his romance with Sheryl had been a casualty. She hadn't been willing to share him—not with his dream and not with his sister. So he'd made his choice, stuck with the plan. All so that he and Marcie could finally be in a position to have everything they ever wanted or needed.

So that Marcie would never want for anything.

Now here they were, fifteen long years later. His company was bordering on going public and his sister was bordering on unwed motherhood.

It wasn't supposed to be like this.

He looked at his watch again.

Lisa returned to call another patient in, this time to room 2. Before Kyle could ask her how much longer this was going to take, she turned toward him and smiled.

"Mr. McDermott?"

He was on his feet instantly.

Lisa opened the door wider and stepped back. "Dr. Maitland says you can come in now."

"How very gracious of her."

Passing the nurse, Kyle struggled to curb his temper. It wasn't the doctor's fault that Marcie had gotten herself pregnant. And it wasn't her fault that Marcie adamantly refused to marry the boy who had gotten her into this condition, despite all Kyle's assurances that he would set them up and help pay for her education and Billy Madison's, as well. But it *was* the doctor's fault that he was now drastically behind schedule. He didn't tolerate lateness well, not in himself and not in others. That wasn't how things got done.

His father had always been late. Late to work, late to pay the bills. Late with everything. That's why he had never amounted to anything, and why, when he died, there had been a mountain of debts for Kyle to pay off.

He walked into room 1 to see his sister lying on the examining table. A wave of discomfort washed over him. His eyes darted toward the doctor. "Is this going to take long?"

Busy preparing the monitor, Abby glanced in his direction. "Not too."

Maybe it was the tension of thinking that one of her brothers might be responsible for the baby she'd just left with Ford. Or maybe it was knowing that, at the very least, because of this baby her family had suddenly become the target of every journalist, photographer and news media wanna-be.

Or maybe she just didn't like Kyle McDermott's distant attitude. Marcie had confided a few things to Abby in moments of dire unhappiness. Things that hadn't put the too-too-busy Mr. McDermott in the most flattering light, despite his chiseled, killer looks, his high cheekbones and that dark, flowing mane of hair that seemed just a bit out of place when paired with the expensive suit he had on.

Whatever it was, Abby found herself hanging on to the tattered ends of a far shorter temper than she normally possessed.

The monitor was ready. She walked over to Marcie, but she was still looking at Kyle.

"Most people view this as a miracle, Mr. McDermott, one not to be hurried through like a car wash. This is a very precious time. You get to make the baby go where you want it to and do what you want it to—except for kicking," she added with a smile as she looked at Marcie. "They really don't listen when it comes to that, no matter what diplomacy you use."

Marcie's swollen abdomen was partially exposed, and Kyle watched as the doctor with the sharp tongue rubbed some sort of jelly on it. He loved Marcie more than anything in this world and had thought, until this thing with Billy had come up, that he was pretty much privy to all her feelings. But right now he felt intrusive, as if he were somehow invading her privacy. It was the same at the birthing classes. He was out of his depth, had no business being there.

Kyle turned away, not sure where he should look.

As she watched him, Abby's lips twitched in amusement. He certainly didn't look like the delicate type.

Can't tell a book by its dust jacket.

Kyle shoved his hands into his pockets and addressed the wall beyond Abby's head. "I don't mean to sound as if this isn't important to me, it's just that—"

"You're running behind schedule, yes, I know." This man was flirting with an ulcer, if he didn't already have one. But that was his problem, not hers. "You made that very clear. I'm afraid most of us are running behind schedule practically from the day we're born. I suspect your niece or nephew might be a few days behind schedule, too." Amplifier in hand, she looked at him. "Ready?"

Kyle really didn't know if he was or not. He knew it was absurd, but he felt nervous about this. That was why he'd turned down Marcie's previous requests to come with her to the doctor's office. But after the argument they'd had last night, he knew this was the only way she would even speak to him.

Masking his emotions, he nodded. "Yes."

Abby placed the amplifier against Marcie's abdomen and began to slowly move it around.

Straining to catch the faintest sound, he heard nothing. Was there something wrong with the baby? Concern edged out discomfort.

"I don't hear anything," Kyle said.

Brows drawn together in concentration, Abby held up her hand for silence. "Wait." And then a smile like late-summer sunshine curved her mouth. Triumph filled her eyes as she looked up at him. "There. Now listen."

He drew his eyes away from her, because she was none of his concern. He was only here because of Marcie. A strange bittersweet emotion filtered through him as he listened. He'd watched Marcie's small body become progressively wider and thicker with child, and yet, somehow, it had all seemed like a fantasy.

Until now. Now there was a heartbeat, and he heard it.

Perhaps that was why he'd resisted this meeting so much, even though he had reluctantly begun accompanying Marcie to her birthing classes, going there in place of Billy, whom he would have thought the more likely choice. Because hearing made it real.

He realized that Marcie's doctor was waiting for him to acknowledge what he heard. He lifted a shoulder and let it drop, not really sure what she wanted from him. ''Sounds like hoofbeats.''

Abby paused, rolling his words over in her mind. She listened closely herself. She'd been doing this for a while now, but had never thought of the sound she was monitoring quite that way. The description made her smile.

''I suppose, in a way, it does.'' Satisfied that everything was fine, Abby put the probe back into place and moved the monitor aside. ''And the beats are getting closer.'' Positioning herself beside Marcie, she gently helped the girl into a sitting position. ''Not much longer now, Marcie-girl.''

The familiar nickname gave testimony to the bond between Marcie and her doctor, and cinched the silent debate Kyle had been having with himself ever since the drive over here. It was very clear to him that he wasn't getting anywhere with Marcie in his campaign. He wanted to convince her to give her child a last name and marry the boy she professed to love so much. Billy was more than willing to marry her, but that didn't seem to be enough to sway Marcie. She was perversely adamant in her refusal, and Kyle could only conclude that she was doing it strictly to annoy him.

But he only wanted what was good for Marcie and he wasn't about to allow her to cut off her nose to spite her face—and him. Not for the first time, he wondered what had become of the little girl who had been his faithful shadow, who had tried so hard to please him. Who'd been so afraid that he would die, too, and leave her alone in the world.

Now she didn't seem to care what he thought.

Maybe this doctor of hers could accomplish what he couldn't. He didn't care how it came about, as long as it did.

"Okay, Marcie, you're doing great," Abby said, making a final notation in her chart. "All systems are go." She flipped the chart closed. "Continue taking your vitamins, get plenty of rest, and I'll see you next week."

But as Abby began to leave, Kyle took her arm, stopping her. She raised her eyes to his quizzically. Was there something she hadn't covered to his satisfaction?

He dropped his hand when she looked at him. Without meaning to, Kyle lowered his voice. It seemed to rumble as it met her ear. "Doctor, could I see you alone for a minute?"

To his surprise and no small annoyance, since she had been the one to keep them waiting, the doctor glanced at her watch. There was just the slightest hint of an apology in her voice.

"I'm afraid it'll have to be just for that one minute. As you pointed out, we're both running behind, and I'm sure you noticed all those women in the waiting room."

This wasn't going to get said in a minute, and he had enough pressure on him without being timed by a woman who barely came up to his shoulder. Kyle bit back the urge to point out that if *she* hadn't come in forty-five minutes late, she wouldn't be so far behind and might have a few minutes to spare for reasonable requests.

He thought a moment. "All right, after hours, then." For a change, he had some time to himself this evening. "What time do you get through?"

He made it sound as if she were a worker on an assembly line, Abby thought, able to tell him when she knocked off for the night. She supposed that to a man who, according to the business section in the *Herald,* was on his way to becoming Austin's next billionaire, she probably was.

She sank her hands into the lab coat's deep pockets. "The posted hours on the door say five o'clock." She'd never shut her doors at that time, even on the first day. "With luck, six."

Kyle nodded. That worked out perfectly. His last meeting was at four. Barring something unforeseen occurring, he should be finished around five-thirty. Even given the traffic at that hour, he could probably make it back here before she had a chance to escape. He had a feeling that consultations with her patients' older brothers were not a high priority with the woman.

"Fine, I can be here by six-thirty. That should give you a little time to catch your breath."

His phrasing seemed to amuse her. Despite her hurry, she paused at the door. "Will I be needing to catch my breath?"

He ignored the strange sensation that ran through him as he watched a quirky smile lift the corners of her generous mouth. At a loss as to how to answer her, he plowed ahead as if she hadn't asked. "There's something I need to discuss with you."

After getting off the table with some difficulty, Marcie combed her fingers through her flattened hair. "He's going to try to get you on his side."

"Side?" For Marcie's sake, Abby gave no indication that she knew anything about the ongoing argument between the girl and her brother. She had a feeling that Kyle McDermott didn't take kindly to people being privy to what went on in his home behind closed doors. She looked at Kyle now, pretending to wait for enlightenment. "As in a debate?"

"As in railroading," Marcie muttered resentfully. Obviously frustrated, she tried to jam her swollen feet into her shoes. The dark flats slid to the side, foiling her efforts.

Kyle bent down, captured her shoes and helped her on with them, Abby noted. He seemed to do it without conscious thought, as if helping Marcie was automatic.

Watching, Abby changed her mind about the refusal that was on the tip of her tongue. At least the man had some redeeming qualities. "Six-thirty it is. Now, if you'll excuse me—"

She was gone before Kyle could say anything more.

"GOT ONE FOR YOU, Daisy."

The matronly-looking woman glanced up from her desk at the police officer ushering the young waif into Serenity Shelter's tiny office.

The older woman's face was lined, but her soft brown eyes were kind and she smiled in response to the policeman's words as she rose from behind her desk. "So, where did you find this one, Rick?"

Rick hooked his thumbs onto his belt as if he wasn't

sure what to do with his hands. "In an alley. She was wandering around, dazed."

Daisy sighed, nodding her head. She peered closer, drawn by the bruises that were just beginning to form. "What's your name, lamb?"

The policeman answered for her. "She doesn't know her name."

Daisy's eyebrows puckered closer together over a remarkably thin nose. She lowered her voice. "Something wrong with her?"

Rick shrugged, the helpless feeling growing. The young woman he'd found turned to look at him without saying a word. She'd been quiet all the way over here. Quiet on the way to the police station, as well. He supposed losing her memory didn't leave her with a whole lot to say.

"There's a bump on her forehead, just where her hair falls over it." He nodded vaguely in her general direction. "Maybe that did it." He sucked air in through his teeth. "She says she can't remember anything."

"I can't," she said softly.

Daisy believed her. The young woman looked as if the sound of her own voice surprised her. Daisy had never had any children of her own. Everyone who passed through the doors of Serenity Shelter was her child. Compassion filled her as she slipped a wide arm around the young woman's small shoulders.

"Don't you worry none—it'll come back to you. But for now, you need a name." Cocking her head, Daisy looked at her, trying to see beyond the bruises. Trying not to judge whoever had given them to her. That wasn't her job. "You look a little like my niece, Sara. How about I call you Sara? Would that be all right with you?"

Newly christened Sara nodded her consent.

That settled, there was more. "Has she been seen by a doctor?"

Rick shook his head. "When I checked her for priors and came up empty, I was going to send her to the clinic." He hesitated. This went beyond duty, but sometimes you had to. "But I thought, in view of the circumstances, maybe you'd want to take her there yourself."

Daisy snorted. "Checked her for priors, indeed. A sweet-faced little thing like this? Anyone with eyes can see how innocent she is." And then she nodded. "Yeah, I guess I've got time to take her to the clinic. In between my pedicure and my massage." The sound emitting from her lips was more of a crackle than a chuckle. "Let's get you checked out, honey, and then we'll see where we can fit you in."

Nowhere, Sara thought. *I fit in nowhere.* She looked at them. They meant well, these people, but they had no idea how it felt to have nothing to think about, nothing to remember.

Daisy reached for her purse in the bottom drawer of her desk, then paused. She saw the look in Sara's eyes. "It'll come back to you. Whatever brought you here, it'll come back." She nodded at Rick, who then took his leave. "You don't know how lucky you are, not remembering. Some of the stories I could tell you..."

Sara didn't feel very lucky. The only feeling she had was a vague sense that something was missing. Something vital. Because there was nothing else, she clung to that as she allowed herself to be ushered out into a world she didn't recognize.

DRAINED, ABBY DROPPED into her chair. The last patient had finally left several minutes ago. She heard the front door close, telling her that Lisa was hurrying home to her twin boys. They'd packed a lot of work into one day. It was 6:19, and they had seen their full load, plus two unexpected patients who'd pleaded emergencies in order to see her. And Mrs. Calvert had had her triplets two weeks early, to add to the excitement of the day.

Abby wondered if it was poor form just to curl up on one of her examination tables and go to sleep.

"You're not getting enough vitamins, Abby-girl," she murmured to herself, trying to summon enough strength to get back on her feet again.

She needn't have bothered. At 6:20, the telephone rang. The flashing red light told her it was coming in on her personal line. Abby pulled the last remaining pin from her hair, and it came tumbling down her back as she reached for the receiver. At least it wouldn't be a prospective father calling her to frantically proclaim, "It's time." Given her druthers, she really didn't want to have to face another woman in the throes of labor tonight.

Taking a deep breath, she brought the receiver to her ear. "Abby."

"Abby, it's Mother. Put on that little television set you have in your office and turn to channel eight."

Her mother rarely called her at work, and when she did, it wasn't to tell her to watch something on television. This wasn't going to be good.

Opening her side drawer to retrieve the remote control, Abby braced herself. "I take it by your tone, I'm not about to be entertained." She aimed the remote at the set and pressed the power button.

"Only if your sense of humor has suddenly turned bizarre."

From the sound of it, her mother was struggling to keep a tight rein on her emotions. Concern took a firmer hold on Abby.

The color on the set came into focus. Flipping quickly, she found Channel 8 and the program that had prompted her mother to call her.

"Son of a gun."

There, smiling up into the camera, was Chelsea Markum—the reporter Abby had taken the baby from this morning. Along the bottom of the screen scrolled the teaser: "Which of the Maitland Men Sired This Baby?" Beside the reporter was a fuzzy photograph of the baby, obviously lifted and freeze-framed from the video taken earlier.

Stifling an exasperated sigh, Abby leaned forward and turned up the sound.

"...Just as the Maitlands' PR department released word of a silver anniversary party in the works to celebrate the clinic's twenty-five years of service, we finally learn that there are skeletons in the very proper Maitland closet, after all. No matter how well respected the family, they obviously have something to hide. Something they're not proud of. So the question still remains—"

Annoyed, Abby turned off the television set. "Ignore it, Mother."

Her mother's voice was calmly logical. "How do I ignore the baby?"

The tension headache that had been building all day now threatened to take Abby's head off. She pressed her fingers to both temples and massaged, knowing it wouldn't help. "Good point."

"I'm calling a family conference tonight." Megan had always been in tune with her children, so her next words came as no surprise to Abby. "If you're too tired…"

She was, but she also knew that she had to be there. This was serious and it affected them all. Abby pushed away from the desk. "No, I'll be there." With effort, she tried to sound brighter. "I just saw my last patient a few minutes ago and I'm free for the evening. I can be at the house in about twenty minutes."

"I appreciate it."

Abby could hear the relief in her mother's voice. "See you."

She hung up, then suddenly remembered that despite what she'd said to her mother, she wasn't free. Marcie McDermott's brother was coming to try to browbeat her into doing heaven only knew what.

"Not tonight, McDermott," she murmured.

But as she reached for the telephone, Abby realized that she had no idea what his number was. He'd failed to give her his card. Probably to avoid having the appointment called off, she thought, getting to her feet.

Maybe the number was in Marcie's file. Lisa had been too busy today to take care of the filing. That meant the files were still stacked on the side of her desk in the order the patients had been seen. Marcie's would be on the bottom.

As she went into the outer office, now dim and eerily still after all the life that had crossed its floors today, a knock on the door startled Abby.

Crossing to it, she saw the outline of someone tall and broad-shouldered through the frosted glass.

McDermott.

"Speak of the devil," she murmured to herself.

CHAPTER THREE

SHE LOOKED HARRIED, Kyle thought, when Abby opened the door to admit him. And her eyes looked tired. The kind of tired that came from juggling too many balls at the same time.

He'd seen the same look staring back at him from the mirror.

Would that work to his benefit or not? Would she give in quickly because she was tired, or would it make her irritable and resistant? He was hoping for the former. The argument he'd had with Marcie on the way home nearly nine hours ago was still fresh in his mind. That about filled his quota for the day. Lately, all Marcie did was argue with him, if she spoke to him at all.

He noticed that Abby wasn't moving aside to let him enter. Behind her, the office was in semidarkness.

"I'm early," he told her.

That was probably meant to be another crack about her arriving late this morning, Abby figured. The smile she forced to her lips was as fake as the Monopoly money she used to play with as a child. "I'm sorry but I'm fresh out of roses to pin on you."

So it was going to be like that, was it? "I'm not interested in roses, Doctor, I'm interested in your support."

"So I gather." Abby leaned against the door she was holding ajar. "Listen, Mr. McDermott—" She paused a second, pressing her lips together. There was a pithy way to phrase this, but for the life of her, she couldn't summon the energy to think of it. She just wanted him to go away. "I know I said that I would see you after hours, but I'm afraid something's come up."

Kyle hadn't gotten where he was in life by allowing himself to be summarily brushed aside. "What?"

His question took Abby by surprise. Someone else would have told him it was none of his business, or hidden behind the convenient excuse that there was a baby on the way and she had to rush off to deliver it.

But Abby didn't like evasion and she liked lying even less. Living by the "do unto others" edict that had been so firmly impressed upon her as a child, she had no option but to tell him the truth.

She didn't have to be friendly about it, though.

"If you must know, I've been called to the house for a family meeting."

"You hold meetings?" He didn't know all that much about the Maitlands, only what he read in passing, and by reputation. He wondered if they were all cold, passionless people who were emotionally distant from one another. It would seem logical that they would be, if family get-togethers were referred to as "meetings."

Though normally easygoing, Abby felt herself taking offense at the tone he used. What right did he have to question her or her family? "We do when there are babies dropped on our doorstep and fingers pointed at us."

Kyle stared at her. "You lost me." He'd had no opportunity to listen to the radio on his way over; he'd been dictating a letter. He had no idea what she meant.

"No, but I'm trying to." With a toss of her head, she

turned on her heel. Walking back to her office, she shed her lab coat as she went.

Kyle followed. She wasn't wearing the suit jacket he'd seen her in earlier, he thought. And she'd done something to her hair. Let it down. It made her look younger. Softer.

He couldn't help noticing, when she swung around again to face him, that the beige turtleneck sweater she had on clung very appealingly to her breasts. Especially as she drew in a deep breath. He realized that he was staring and raised his eyes to her face again.

She should have just politely shut the door on him, Abby thought. She wasn't any good at excuses. "I know that this must seem like I'm trying to brush you off—"

"Good call."

Kyle knew she was going to try to make it a done deal if he didn't say something to stop her. He needed this woman backing him up if he was going to have a prayer of convincing Marcie to be sensible. It wasn't hard to see that his sister thought the world of Abby Maitland. The woman was the first role model Marcie had turned to since…he couldn't remember when.

Sensing that she was a person who could be appealed to on an emotional level, he went that way. "Look, Doctor, it might not seem like it to you, but I really love my sister and I only want what's best for her."

Given her track record as far as men went, Abby knew that she wasn't always the best judge of character when it came to the opposite sex. But she believed he was sincere. Or at the very least, that he believed himself to be sincere. He'd proven that by making time in the "busy schedule" Marcie had complained to her about. And there was the matter of the birthing classes.

Marcie had signed her brother up as her partner. It spoke to Abby of a strong bond, no matter what words might be flying around to the contrary.

That all counted for something.

Tossing her lab coat over the back of her chair, she reached for her jacket and proceeded to put it on. ''Yes, I believe that you do.'' The right sleeve was giving her trouble as she tried to push her arm through. Par for the course today, she thought. ''But I really do have to be at my mother's…''

Her voice trailed off as she felt a pair of strong, masculine hands easing the jacket onto her shoulders. She hadn't even realized that he'd moved behind her. Something akin to a misty premonition zigzagged through her before vanishing. She hadn't a clue what that was all about, and had less than no time to ponder it.

Turning around, Abby found herself a hairbreadth away from him. Surprised, she felt a spike of adrenaline shoot through her. The pounding in her head increased, and she winced involuntarily.

He saw the pain in her a second before she winced. ''What's the matter?''

''Tension headache.'' A vague shrug accompanied the confession she knew she should have kept to herself. She wasn't a complainer by nature. Not even when her heart was hurt. No one in the family had any idea just how deeply she'd been wounded by Drew Brandon's duplicity. It was something that, for the most part, she kept to herself. Only a couple of her friends even came close to suspecting the extent of the damage Drew and his womanizing had done.

The familiar term evoked a half smile. Kyle nodded in mute sympathy. ''Had more than my share of tension headaches. Sit down.''

Where did he get off ordering her around? Abby raised her chin. "I don't have—"

He was beginning to see what it was about Abby Maitland that Marcie related to so well. They both appeared to be stubborn as hell. Resting his hands on her shoulders, he gently but firmly pushed her down into the chair. She glared up at him with eyes that were accusing and wary at the same time.

Did she think she had something to fear from him? The thought surprised him. He could handle himself in any given situation, physical or otherwise, but it had never occurred to him to use anything but his powers of persuasion when it came to women.

Kyle purposely made his voice calm and reasonable. "As you pointed out, we're all running behind from the moment we're born. A couple more minutes won't put you much further in the red." So saying, he turned her chair around so that her back was to him.

He noted that she perched more than sat—probably debating whether to bolt, he decided.

This served her right for agreeing to see him after hours, Abby thought, annoyed at her carelessness. As the daughter of wealthy parents, she knew all the precautions she was supposed to take. But she often thought of them as imprisoning her rather than keeping her safe, and she tended to be lax, preferring to think of everyone as nonthreatening.

She wasn't all that sure about Marcie's older brother, however. *Nonthreatening* wasn't a word she would have equated with Kyle McDermott.

She felt his hands on her shoulders again, just shy of her neck. Strong, powerful hands. Hands that could easily do damage, given cause. Stiffening, she tried to rise. "I really don't—"

The last words of the sentence failed to emerge as a shock wave shot through the top of her head in response to the pressure he was applying to the knotted muscles of her shoulders. A slight gasp escaped before she could stop it.

A whisper of guilt slipped through Kyle at the sound. He wasn't trying to hurt her. "It'll probably feel worse before it starts to feel better," he warned, working his fingers farther into the rigid area.

"Too late." She tried to brace herself and found that she couldn't. All she could do was hold on and hope she didn't make a fool of herself. "I think you just took off the top of my skull."

Abby felt his hard torso against her back as he leaned forward, inspecting the area in question. She could have sworn she felt his breath move along the suddenly sensitized flesh beneath her hair.

"Nope, it's still there."

"Good," she said, exhaling slowly. Why was her pulse suddenly racing? Her brother Mitchell had warned her about pacing herself and working too hard. She should have listened to him. She was paying the price for that now.

"I've gotten very attached to it," Abby heard herself say.

Like thick molasses, relief moved slowly along the shoulders he was kneading up to her neck, then made its way by micro-steps to her temples. Stunned, surprised and feeling strangely light-headed, Abby took a deep breath, held it, then let it out slowly.

"Better?"

The question seemed to drift to her out of nowhere, parting a haze as it came. "Yes. A little." With effort, she forced herself to turn the chair to face him, though the magic the man performed was seductive.

As was the feel of his hands on her shoulders.

Abby raised her eyes to his, trying not to cling to the sensation he'd created. "And that's all I'm going to have time for."

Kyle had no idea why a smile was forming within him. He'd come here to make his arguments, to win her over to his way of thinking. Humor had no place in this; the issue was too important. And yet here he was, smiling at her for expressing the same sentiments that drove him.

"Afraid they'll start the meeting without you?" He echoed the question that Marcie had accusingly put to him earlier, momentarily seeing her side of it.

Abby found that she had to grip the armrests to get herself up. She felt like warm liquid seeking a vessel to rest in. But at least the tension headache was miraculously gone. Her eyes held his, and despite herself she was fascinated by the half smile.

"Someone pointed out to me today that it's disrespectful to be late."

She was tossing his words back at him. Odd that he didn't mind. Kyle inclined his head. "You're a quick study."

"Whenever possible." On her feet again, telling herself that the wobbly feeling in her thighs was a result of not finishing the single sandwich she'd allowed herself for lunch, Abby hesitated as she studied Kyle's expression. Damn it, but she truly did believe he was sincere. "If this is really that important to you, you're welcome to follow me to the house and wait in the library until I'm free. With luck, it won't take too long."

Tacitly, Kyle accepted the invitation, knowing it was not a choice. "I get the feeling that there's no other way to see you except on your terms."

He made it sound as if she were drafting a treaty. "I don't have terms, Mr. McDermott. I just have a very busy life." She pulled open the bottom drawer. "Take it or leave it."

"I'll take it."

Abby raised her eyes until they met his. He surprised her. She hadn't really thought that he would agree; it was just an offer she felt compelled to make because he had vanquished her tension headache. And because he'd looked, for just a moment, like a determined white knight.

She was far too easygoing for her own good, she chided herself. But now that she'd made the offer, she knew she couldn't very well rescind it. That wouldn't be playing fair.

With a sigh, she pulled her purse out of the drawer and let the drawer slide back into place. "All right, the address is—"

That she felt she had to actually give it to him amused Kyle. "Everyone knows where Maitland Mansion is." What went unsaid was that, as a teenager, he used to drive by the estate in his second-hand car whenever the opportunity presented itself, vowing that someday he'd have a mansion just like it. And a life just like the Maitlands'. A life that commanded respect.

"All right, then." Resigned, she led the way out. "Let's go."

SHE DROVE TOO FAST, Kyle thought, following Abby's bright red Jaguar up the winding hill that led to her family's estate. He wondered if her speed was a natural outpouring of residual energy, or if she just had an incredibly heavy foot.

Or maybe she was trying to lose him.

In any case, a doctor should have known better than to drive like that. She didn't weave in and out of traffic, but that was only because there was no other traffic.

He decided that being in a hurry was a natural part of Abby Maitland's makeup.

The Maitland estate was located a mere ten blocks from the clinic, but upon driving into the compound, housed behind tall, imposing electronic black gates, Kyle felt as if they had entered another world. In the distance, the stately white house rose up in front of him. Four sprawling floors reaching up to the sky beneath a light clay-tiled roof that seemed more reminiscent of an old English castle than a Texas mansion.

There was a guest cottage on the premises, barely visible off to the side. Hidden from view were the tennis court and the pool that Kyle knew were located at the rear of the property. The tennis court alone was larger than the lot on which his boyhood home had stood.

The rich sure knew how to live, he thought. It was a talent he was still trying to acquire. But work kept getting in the way. Another skill he had yet to acquire, he knew, was the ability to delegate. But he couldn't overcome the nagging fear that if he wasn't involved in all phases of operation, everything would break down and come to a grinding halt. Being on the leading edge of communications technology meant never slowing your pace.

It looked as if Abby hadn't been blowing him off about the "meeting," after all, Kyle thought as they approached the mansion. There was a squadron of cars parked in the circular gray-and-white paved driveway.

He quickly surveyed the various makes and models. They would make an automobile aficionado drool.

It was difficult not to feel out of place, even behind the wheel of a Mercedes. He supposed that was because no matter what the numbers on the ledgers said, deep down he was still that scrawny, awkward kid in his cousin's hand-me-downs.

Kyle was beginning to have doubts that he would ever be entirely free of that image.

But for now, he pushed that negative thought aside, just as he had countless other times during the early years of his business when all his efforts looked as if they might blow up in his face. It had taken fierce determination for him to believe in himself, but it had paid off.

He was as good as any of these people, Kyle told himself. He just had to hold on to that thought.

After pulling up beside Abby's car, Kyle turned off the engine and got out quickly. Abby was already ahead of him, waiting on the bottom of the steps that led up to the massive front door. Kyle lengthened his stride, sensing she would only wait a moment. "You drive too fast."

The blunt observation surprised Abby. People who wanted to win you over to their side didn't start out by admonishing you. It seemed the man was full of contradictions. He was also undoubtedly accustomed to getting his way, if not through sheer force of will, then by his looks. She found herself wondering if any woman had ever said no to him—and meant it.

"So my brothers say," she acknowledged, inclining her head. "I tend to do that when I'm running behind." The look she gave him was long, penetrating and deep. "I'm sure someone like you can understand that."

He could, but he also knew better. Life had taught him that. "Better late than never," he countered. When she raised a quizzical brow, he added, "My mother drove like you do. She died in a car crash a little more than sixteen years ago."

Caught unprepared, Abby could only murmur, "I'm sorry."

He said nothing, merely shrugged as he fell in beside her. There was no point in going over what was in the past and couldn't be changed. He was interested in the present, and how it could influence the future.

Kyle drank in the splendor that was Maitland Mansion. The word *grand* seemed hopelessly insufficient. It took him back to the boy he'd been. The dreamer. "I've always wondered what it looked like inside."

The admission made Abby smile. He probably didn't realize that he sounded almost wistful. Taking the lead, she hurried up the steps. "Then wonder no more."

She rang the doorbell even though she had a key. Harold would be there to open the front door before she ever located her key within the jumble of her purse.

The stern face that appeared when the door was opened broke into a wreath of smiles as recognition sank in. Clear blue eyes crinkled with pleasure. "Miss Abby, how nice to see you again."

She could remember a time when the tall, stately man had seemed larger than life to her. Now there was a touch of frailty hovering over him that tugged on her heart strings. "Hello, Harold."

She surprised Kyle by brushing her lips over the butler's cheek. The pale complexion grew pink where her lips had touched it.

"Am I the last one?" she asked, walking in.

Harold nodded. "They're all in the living room." He

inclined his head in that general direction, but his eyes rested on Kyle. There was not even the slightest spark of curiosity in them. To Harold, curiosity was a plebeian sentiment. What he needed to know he would be told, by and by.

Abby glanced toward the living room. The doors were closed. Not a good sign. She wondered if anything had been decided yet.

The slight, almost imperceptible clearing of a throat made her remember the man at her side. And her manners. "This is Kyle McDermott. Mr. McDermott, this is Harold, without whom everything in the Maitland household would fall to pieces."

The modest smile threatened to take possession of the butler's entire face. "You flatter me, Miss Abby."

She caught the old man's arm in a quick, affectionate embrace. "Not nearly enough." She released her hold. Time to see what was going on. "Please show Mr. McDermott to the library, Harold." She spared Kyle a quick glance. "I'll be there as soon as I can."

"I'll be waiting."

"I'm sure you will," she murmured, hurrying away.

Kyle watched her for a second, noting that the gentle sway of her hips increased as she picked up speed.

"This way, sir."

It sounded more like a command than a request. Turning away, Kyle followed the older man.

The butler was silent as he led the way down a hallway discreetly showcasing fine sculptures and paintings that looked vaguely familiar from an art history course dating back to Kyle's freshman year in college.

He wondered if he should be dropping bread crumbs to help him find his way back, in case the good doctor forgot about him. He would have been willing to bet that more than one person had gotten lost here.

"May I bring you some refreshments?" Harold asked as he opened the double doors that led into the library.

The room more than deserved its name. The mingled scent of lemon oil, leather and roses greeted him. For a moment, Kyle didn't acknowledge the butler's question, as he looked around the room. It rose two stories, with books residing on dark oak shelves that completely lined three of its walls. In the rear of the library, stairs led to an alcove that housed more books and a long table.

Had Abby done her studying here? Kyle wondered. Or was this all for show? "Quite impressive."

"The Maitlands all like to read, sir. Some of the books here are over two hundred years old," Harold told him. "About the refreshments?" A gray brow rose.

Kyle shook his head, still looking around. "Nothing for me, thanks."

Harold remained standing where he was. "It might be a while, sir."

Kyle looked at the man, feeling as if he had been given a subtle hint. "In that case, make it a scotch. Neat."

A small smile played along the very thin lips. "We're never messy here, sir." With that, Harold turned and discreetly faded, more than walked, from the room. He closed the doors behind him.

Was that for privacy, or to seal him in? Kyle had a feeling it was the latter.

Over the years Kyle had found that the kind of books people kept on their shelves gave him useful insight into the people themselves. So, with nothing else to do, he began reading the lettering along the leather spines.

CHAPTER FOUR

ABBY EASED THE DOORS shut behind her. "Sorry I'm late, everybody." She went no further with her excuse. There was no point, for the moment. Kyle McDermott's presence in the house had no bearing on this meeting.

Her mother was on the sofa, with Beth and Ellie on either side of her. Like a tribunal, Abby thought, amused at the image. Both girls looked like a younger version of their mother. Photographs of Megan Maitland at twenty-five bore that out.

Crossing to her mother, Abby bent and kissed Megan's cheek. "So, did I miss anything?" She purposely infused her voice with a cheeriness she didn't quite feel.

"Nothing more than the rest of us," R.J. told her tersely. His glass empty, he turned toward the decanter on the bar for a refill.

He was drinking his whiskey straight tonight, Abby noted. R.J. rarely drank at all. Was the unexpected appearance of this baby responsible? Or was it just, as in her case, general tension that forced him to seek any kind of relief?

Anna, the oldest of the Maitland daughters, came up behind her to hand her a glass of wine.

Abby shook her head, passing. "I have that and I'll fall asleep before anyone says anything."

"I doubt that."

Nonetheless, Anna set the glass down on the bar and

picked up her own goblet of wine. She looked around the room, her eyes coming to rest on Megan. Though they didn't share the same blood, no daughter could love a mother more, Abby thought.

Though obviously worried about how this would all effect Megan, Anna struggled to force a brave smile to her lips. "I doubt any of us will get much sleep for at least the next few days to come."

Megan drew herself up, bracing for the unpleasant task before her.

"I think we should get to the heart of this matter as quickly as possible, and I felt it was something we needed to do in person." Her eyes swept over her children. They were a close unit, and nothing was going to change that. "As uncomfortable as this is for me to ask, is either one of you responsible for this child?"

Her gaze came to rest on R.J. and Mitchell. She'd always liked to believe that she was a good mother, a kind mother, with an endless supply of love, understanding and support for all her children. Because of this, she required—and got—nothing but the truth from them.

She wanted the truth now.

R.J. cleared his throat and regarded his drink. The slight hint of color that rose to Mitchell's face aroused Megan's curiosity. Older than Abby by two years, Mitchell had gone into science. Now a fertility specialist, he had, like his siblings, dedicated his talents to the clinic.

Megan began with him. "Mitchell?"

He shook his head, a rueful smile on his lips, a touch of embarrassment in his eyes. "Not me, Mother. In fact, this isn't the kind of thing that a fertility specialist would like to have get around, but I haven't been with a woman for over a year.'' He took the last sip of his drink, then put the glass down. ''The only way that baby is mine is if there's been another case of divine intervention.''

Megan shifted her gaze to R.J.

He looked more than mildly uncomfortable, Abby thought. Just as he had earlier this morning. Was that guilt, or only R.J.'s displeasure at having the family name dragged through the mud?

''It's not mine,'' he finally said. But his voice didn't carry its customary conviction.

Beth exchanged a look with Ellie, but neither said a word. And then Mitchell said aloud what they were all thinking. ''That leaves us with Jake.''

''If the baby really *is* a Maitland, then Jake's the most likely candidate,'' Abby reluctantly agreed. Jake was her younger brother and she loved him dearly, but there was no denying that he'd distanced himself from the family. He was the only one—other than Anna, who was a wedding planner—who didn't work for the family in some capacity. ''Nobody knows where he is.''

''Or what he does for a living,'' Anna added. Jake was the family's man of mystery, slipping in and out of their lives like an evening breeze.

''No,'' Megan pointed out, ''that doesn't leave us with only Jake.'' The others all turned to look at her. ''Of course, he's a strong possibility, but there are other Maitland men to consider, if in name only.''

R.J.'s expression brightened a little, and if Abby hadn't known any better, she would have said he looked almost hopeful.

''You mean Connor, don't you?'' he asked.

They all knew about Connor O'Hara, though not even their mother had seen him since he'd been a boy of three. Connor was the adopted son of their father's sister, Clarise, and her husband, Jack. The O'Hara family had become estranged from the rest of the Maitlands after a petty misunderstanding between William and Jack some forty-three years ago. Since then, there had been no contact between the families, not even after William's death.

Megan inclined her head. "Yes, and there's one more possibility." It pained her to bring this up because she wasn't sure how the reminder might affect R.J. and Anna, but they had to be aware of all avenues and take them into consideration. "We don't know what became of your father's brother, Robert. He might have remarried or at least had more children—we just don't know."

Tactfully, she refrained from saying that he was actually R.J. and Anna's father. Younger than William and far less stable, Robert had abandoned his two children after the death of his wife. William, with his large heart, had taken them in. R.J. and Anna became their first two children, to be followed by five more.

"So, why don't we hire a detective?" Beth suggested. "Start finding things out?"

Megan thought of the secrets that might be uncovered, secrets that would make them even more vulnerable to the invading press. She really didn't want to go that route—not yet. Not until it was absolutely necessary.

"I'll look into it," she promised evasively, temporarily calling a halt to that line of conversation. At the moment there was something even more important to consider. "All right, for the time being, let's proceed as if this baby actually is a Maitland. We'll keep him at Maitland Maternity for as long as possible."

"Which won't be too long," Abby pointed out. "Ford said the baby is in perfect health." Her mother knew as well as she did what that meant. "Social services will be coming for him."

Unconsciously, Megan straightened her shoulders. "Leave social services to me."

They all knew their mother was more than equal to taking on any agency and coming out on top, never deviating from the rules of fair play. Unfortunately, the social agency wasn't the immediate thorn in their side.

"But how do we stop people like that Markum woman?" R.J. asked.

"We don't stop them," Megan told him. "We ignore them. Breeding will win out in the end."

Abby wished that the situation were as simple as it seemed to her mother. She exchanged glances with her twin sisters. She could see they were of like mind. "In a perfect world, Mother."

Megan remained unfazed. "Honesty and discretion will work in any situation, Abby."

Anna raised her brow in feigned amusement. "Littering doorsteps with unwanted babies is hardly honest or discreet."

Abby took exception to Anna's choice of words. "I don't think the baby isn't wanted. Otherwise, the mother wouldn't have written 'Please take care of him until I can again.' She would have just written, 'Here, take care of him, I can't.'"

"Abby has a point," Ellie agreed.

Abby glanced at her watch. It was getting late. "Abby also has someone waiting for her in the library. He—"

Abruptly, Abby stopped. The moment she'd spoken, she knew she'd made a mistake. Ellie and Beth immediately came to life, and both sets of eyes turned eagerly to inspect her. Anna was only a beat behind, scrutinizing her as if there were encrypted answers in her expression.

"Oh? Who?" Anna asked.

Abby rarely dated and had thwarted numerous attempts on her family's part to set her up with men they considered good possibilities. The fact that she had a living, breathing male stashed away and waiting for her in the library aroused instant interest from all fronts. She knew this had the potential to snowball if she wasn't careful.

"Just the brother of one of my patients." Her tone was casual, dismissive. "I told him to come by the office after hours."

"This is getting more interesting..." Mitchell raised and lowered his brow comically.

Abby sent a withering look his way. She knew their hearts were in the right place. It was their noses she objected to. "You know what I didn't like about growing up in the middle of a big family, Mother?"

Playing along, Megan deadpanned, "No, what, dear?"

"There was never any privacy." Abby's gaze swept over all of them, warning them that she was too tired to put up with teasing comments for very long. "Fortunately, I can walk away now."

"Spoilsport," Beth called after her.

"You bet," Abby shot back over her shoulder, then looked at her mother. "Okay if I leave?"

Megan rose. They'd said all there was to say for the moment. There was one more thing, but she wasn't going to mention it now. For the time being, she intended to keep to herself the baby bracelet she'd taken from the infant with its initials, CO. She'd noticed it when she first saw the baby, and had managed to remove it without anyone observing her doing it.

"Of course. I think this little meeting is at an end, anyway. I appreciate the fact that you all came, even though we're no closer to learning the truth about the baby's parents." Megan hoped that if any of her children did know more than they'd admitted tonight, they would willingly seek her out in private. In any case, her own questioning of them was over.

At the door, Abby turned around to look at her mother. "If you ask me, the butler did it."

"Did what, miss?"

The door had opened and Abby almost stumbled backward, as Harold materialized in front of her. She collected herself quickly.

"Everything, Harold." Hooking her arm through his, she patted his sleeve affectionately. "And you do it so well, too."

"I have help." Harold, of course, was referring to a formidable-looking housekeeper named Dora, and Jessie, the cook.

Priding himself on discretion, he lowered his voice. "I just wanted to stop by and inform you that your young gentleman is falling asleep."

Abby didn't have to look to know that all eyes had focused on her again. She knew any diversion from the problem staring them in the face was welcome, but she didn't care for the fact that she had, by default, become that diversion.

"He's not my young gentleman, Harold, or my young anything. He doesn't belong to me." Knowing the value of a timely retreat, Abby moved quickly into the hallway. "I'll see you at the clinic tomorrow,

Mother," she called over her shoulder. *Hopefully at the beginning of a saner day,* she added silently.

Abby entered the library ahead of Harold, who closed the door silently behind her. If Kyle had been sleeping, he was awake now and in the middle of rotating his shoulders. Probably to rid himself of some ache in his neck, she surmised.

"Sorry to keep you waiting," she apologized, then realized that this was the second time she'd said that to him today. She didn't like apologizing—not when it wasn't her fault. "But it was unavoidable."

He rose from the chair. "Is there anything in your life that *is* avoidable?"

"Until now, I would have said encountering rude people, but I seem to have broken my streak of luck."

Instead of being annoyed, he looked amused. "Family meetings always sharpen your tongue?"

"No, I come that way." She cocked her head, studying him. "Harold said you were falling asleep."

Kyle's first instinct was to deny it, but then he thought better of it. He'd chosen his arguments with her, and this wasn't going to be one of them. "Harold was right. It's been a long day for me." Starting at four-thirty this morning when he'd had to get up for a conference call to Rome. His company was definitely moving up in the world.

"Me, too. So why don't we just table this until some other time?"

Time was running out on him, at least as far as Marcie and her pending motherhood was concerned. "I'm afraid I can't do that."

Even tired, the man was stubborn. Resigned, Abby gestured to the chair he'd just vacated. "All right, let's get to it. You wanted to talk to me. Talk."

He wasn't sure what stopped him. Maybe it was the mood she seemed to be in, or just the way she looked at him. He wasn't going to get anywhere right now. He knew that if he tried to persuade Abby Maitland to side with him here, he'd most likely fail.

But he didn't want to make an appointment for another time. His sister's due date was not all that far away, and appointments could always be broken. Abby had already proven that.

What he needed was home-court advantage, or at least a neutral place. Maitland Mansion could not be thought of as either. Neither could a library conducive to dozing.

"Have you eaten?"

Where had that come from? "Nothing that I remember." Abby drew her brows together. "Why?"

"Because I'd like to take you to dinner."

She looked momentarily nonplussed. "Won't do you any good. The condition of my stomach does not affect the way I think."

Her answer almost made him grin. If he were of a mind to sway her, he'd have resorted to something far more sophisticated than dinner.

"Then that would make you unique. Most people react better to things on a full stomach. Empty ones tend to make them irritable."

"Are you saying I'm irritable?" Abby supposed, in all fairness, that this wasn't one of her better days. But taking everything into consideration, she thought she was doing pretty well.

"I'm saying I like to cover my bets." He looked into her eyes. "Humor me."

It seemed to Abby that he had somehow moved closer to her, though she wasn't aware of just when.

Standing her ground, she returned his steady gaze. "And why should I do that?"

"Because I'm a fair judge of character, and I think you care about Marcie almost as much as I do. Plus, if you have dinner with me, I'll make a sizable donation to the Maitland Maternity Foundation."

This time, her lips curved. She knew all about the semiconductor he had designed on the back of his napkin while doodling in a computer engineering class, and the corporation he'd founded. Marcie had filled her in on the highlights. And the business section of the newspaper rarely missed a mention of Kyle's telecommunications company's latest inventions and its CEO's burgeoning wealth. He could well afford to make sizable donations to a lot of foundations.

"Then you're not above bribery?"

He didn't miss a beat. "Not a whit."

Far be it from Abby to stand in the way of another donation, but she wanted him to have the facts up front. "You realize that all you'd be buying is my time, not my support."

He lifted one shoulder in a careless shrug. "I'll take what I can get."

She was sure he would.

THEY DROVE IN SEPARATE cars because she insisted on it, and met in the parking lot of one of Austin's five-star restaurants, even though Abby would have been just as happy eating in the diner across from Maitland Maternity. Maybe happier. She was used to the food there, and the ambience critics liked to prattle on about came from the people, not any decor flown in from the four corners of the world at an obscene cost. Besides, it would be throwing business Shelby Lord's way, since she owned the diner. And she and Shelby were friends.

As befitted the hour and the restaurant's reputation, the parking lot was more than three-quarters full. So full that there were no two side-by-side spots to be found. Kyle let Abby park first, then hurriedly found a spot for himself, keeping an eye on Abby. She figured he was afraid she might hop back into her car and drive off, and he obviously had no intention of allowing that to happen. He'd invested his time and he meant to get something back for it.

The man was dangerous. The thought telegraphed itself to her out of nowhere as she watched him approach—like a hunter stalking prey.

A shiver went up her spine despite the warm evening.

"Listen, about that donation in exchange for my time," she began as they walked up the steps to the restaurant. "No one's going to hold you to that. I'm willing to do it without having you pay for it."

A couple walking by looked at her. The man who held the door open gave Abby a long once-over.

For the first time, Kyle grinned. "You know what that sounded like to them, don't you?"

She nodded, trying not to be sidetracked by his openly engaging smile. "I know. All I need is for Chelsea Markum to pop out of the woodwork with her camera crew. I can see the next program—'Which Maitland Daughter Earns Her Money as a Part-time Call Girl?'"

Kyle's brow rose slightly. "Chelsea Markum?"

"A reporter on *Tattle Today TV*."

Catching the maître d's eye, Kyle held up two fingers. The man picked up a couple of menus and began walking toward them. "You watch that kind of programming?" Kyle asked.

"I did tonight."

Abby felt the oddest sensation travel through her as Kyle placed his hand on her spine and gently ushered her into the main dining area. Despite her jacket, she could feel each of his fingers against her back. She had to concentrate not to lose her train of thought.

"We were the featured story." She sighed as they came to their table. "Why is it that people are so eager to hear the worst about others?"

Kyle waited until the maître d' finished helping her with her chair, then sat down himself. "Not the worst, maybe, but something that makes deities more like themselves. The Greeks and Romans gave all their gods human failings." Kyle ordered a bottle of wine that would once have represented a week's salary for him, then opened the menu out of habit, scanning it without thinking. He knew what he wanted.

Abby followed suit, but she didn't bother reading. Her attention was focused on the man sitting across from her. Was he trying to flatter her, or was he mocking her? After a few minutes, she remarked, "We're hardly deities. We're just a family."

Kyle leaned back as the maître d' returned with the bottle of wine and began to pour. "Like the Rockefellers and the Fortunes are just a family. Money brings attention and very close scrutiny." He raised his glass to her in a silent toast.

He *was* mocking her, Abby thought. She left her glass standing where it was, pinning Kyle with a look that would have sent a lesser man running. "You didn't ask me out to dinner to talk about my life. Just what is it you want from me, Mr. McDermott?"

Kyle had discovered that he enjoyed wheeling and dealing, and after so much practise, he'd grown very cool under direct fire. Like the fire of a light flashing in a beautiful woman's eyes.

After taking a sip of his wine, he set the glass down on the table. Never flinching, he continued to meet her steady gaze. "Well, for openers, I'd like you to call me Kyle."

"Why, so that this sounds more personal?"

He leaned closer over the table. His answer brought him closer still. "Yes."

Abby took a deep breath, then decided that maybe she could do with some wine, after all. "Well, at least you're honest."

"Whenever possible."

"Meaning that sometimes you're not?"

She was quick. He liked that. It never hurt to admire an adversary, and he had a strong feeling that if he didn't get her to side with him, Abby Maitland would prove to be a very strong adversary.

"Meaning that sometimes honesty hurts." He had no doubt that she'd learned that at an early age.

She thought of Drew, of discovering that he had been interested in her only for her money and for the connections that marriage to a Maitland would bring him. Discovering that truth had hurt incredibly and for a very long time.

Chasing the memory away, she looked at him. "So sometimes you subscribe to the edict that better a gentle lie than the harsh truth?"

What harsh truths had she encountered? Kyle found himself wondering. He would have thought someone like her, born in the lap of luxury, never wanting for anything, would be shielded from things like "harsh truths." "Something like that."

The waiter came to take their order, and Abby ordered the first thing on the list, a seafood pasta, knowing she'd never finish it. Her initial hunger had managed to feed on itself and desert her. She hardly paid attention to what Kyle ordered.

She waited until the waiter left before continuing. She had a feeling that with very little prodding, this discussion could very well go on all night. She didn't have that luxury of time available to her.

"Mr. McDermott—Kyle—I'm much too tired to debate with you. Let's get to the heart of the matter. I'm guessing that you want me to use what you think is my influence with Marcie to get her to what—give up the baby?" It was the first thing that came to mind.

Kyle had considered that option, but only briefly, and solely for Marcie's benefit. "No, although I think adoption might make things easier for Marcie. She's really too young to be a mother." Abby had to see that. Marcie was only eighteen. "She has her whole life in front of her. She should be out, enjoying each stage, not taking on a responsibility she shouldn't even be thinking about for another five, ten years."

Abby wondered if Kyle McDermott mapped everything out in life, or if there was room for spontaneity.

"Life doesn't go according to a schedule," she replied. "Certainly not one I've ever seen." Because there was a constant hum of noise in the restaurant, Abby leaned closer to him across the small table. "You said you thought it might make things easier for Marcie, but there was reservation in your voice. Why?"

It was more than just reservation, he thought. It was objection. "Because I don't know who the baby would go to, and I think that families belong together. To be quite honest—" he smiled "—I don't like the idea of my nephew or niece being raised by strangers."

"They wouldn't be strangers once they adopted the child—they would be parents," Abby reminded him.

He offered her a dinner roll, then took one himself when she declined. "It's a moot point. I don't want her to give the baby up for adoption. I want her to get married to the father of her baby."

From his tone, it wasn't hard to guess the rest. "But Marcie doesn't."

"No, and I don't understand why." Kyle buttered his roll with feeling, transferring some of his frustration to the action. The whole thing mystified him. "She says she loves him. I've offered to set them both up in a place of their own, pay the bills until they're on their feet, even pay for both their education if that's what it takes."

He thought money solved everything, Abby realized. He wasn't alone in his thinking, even though it was so off base. "Very generous. Why is it so important to you that Marcie get married?"

He hadn't expected her to challenge him on this. He would have thought the Maitlands at least paid lip service to traditional beliefs. "Because it's important for a baby to have both parents."

"But the baby *will* have both parents, from what Marcie tells me." She had a feeling that wasn't enough for him. "Just not under the same roof."

"But that's the problem. They should be under one roof. Legally." He'd never gotten ahead by doing things in half measures. "Look, I'm old-fashioned. I believe that if people want to play house and that 'playing' has consequences, then they should do the responsible thing and get married." He thought of the last argument he'd had with Marcie. They'd gone round and round without resolving anything. "Especially if they love each other."

He was for real, wasn't he? Abby didn't know whether to be charmed or annoyed. Was he being chivalrous, or narrow-minded because what Marcie did reflected on him? Cocking her head, she studied him as the wine rippled through her empty stomach, warming it as it went. "How do you feel about shades of gray?"

Right now, he was looking into a compelling shade of blue. Her eyes had seemed light when he'd been in her office this morning; now they were almost navy. Her question faintly buzzing in his head, Kyle roused himself. "What?"

There was something about the way he was looking at her that made her stomach even more unsettled than the wine had. Abby reached for the glass again without thinking, then left it where it was. Instead, she wet her lips. "Not all things are black and white anymore."

He found it just the slightest bit difficult to think when the dimmed lighting seemed to glisten along her lips. "No, but some things are."

For safety's sake, she looked down at her empty bread plate. Because she needed something to do with her hands, she reached for the basket of rolls. He saw what she wanted and was faster, moving the basket toward her. Their fingers touched, and a silent communion that had nothing to do with the discussion took place.

Abby ate the roll without butter and hardly tasted it. "I don't think it's in the interest of your sister's happiness to force her into a situation she doesn't want."

As if he could ever make Marcie do anything. "Not force, just make her see the light."

He could be heavy-handed when it was important.

She had no idea how she knew that about him, but she did. "I'm sure you're flashing it in her eyes, and she still can't see it. Maybe for her, it isn't the light." She paused, wondering how best to make him understand her point without having this escalate. "Let me ask you—if it were you in that situation, would you get married?"

There wasn't a heartbeat's hesitation. He'd already put the same question to himself when he'd found out about Marcie's condition. "If I loved the woman, yes."

Well, that wasn't going the way she'd hoped. "Then, Kyle, you are a very nice man. But—"

The all-powerful three-letter word. *But.* He'd grown to hate it, though it had never stopped him. "You're not going to have that talk with her, are you?"

The smile on her lips was neither dismissive nor apologetic. It just was. And it made her seem...*desirable,* he thought, the word bringing with it a wave of feeling he hadn't experienced in a long time.

"It's not my place."

He differed. "Marcie respects you."

"And I'm flattered. But I wouldn't respect myself if I tried to talk her into doing something she didn't feel was right for her."

He read between the lines. "So you're telling me to butt out."

He obviously loved his sister. Abby could see it in his eyes, and she was happy for the girl. Headstrong and determined, Marcie still needed someone like her brother in her corner. "No, I'm telling you that *I'm* not butting in. What you do is up to you."

She looked at the waiter approaching with their food. Very politely and with an unexpected tinge of regret,

Abby folded her napkin and placed it on the table. "Perhaps you'd like me to leave."

Kyle captured her hand before she could begin to rise. "Not necessarily."

CHAPTER FIVE

ABBY LOOKED AT HIM for what felt like a long moment. Why had he stopped her? As far as she was concerned, this was a thinly veiled business meeting, and business had just been concluded to his dissatisfaction.

Or had it? Marcie had mentioned that Kyle was stubborn. Maybe he was one of those people who lived by the axiom "Never say die." In that case, she'd better make things clear to him.

"I just told you that I'm not about to get in the middle of this, other than to tell you that I think Marcie is rather mature for her age."

She saw by the momentary shift in his expression that Kyle didn't agree with her. But then, she hadn't expected him to. He was too close to this.

And right now, to her. Deliberately, she freed her wrist from his hand. "There's no need to continue with dinner. You don't have to pretend to be polite."

The smile on his lips filtered into his eyes. "I don't 'pretend' to be polite, Doctor. I am. Sometimes so polite, it hurts." Otherwise, Marcie's Billy would have had to learn how to live life as a pretzel when Kyle had found out the boy had been intimate with her. "Now, I said I'd buy you dinner, and I intend to do just that. What you do with that dinner once it arrives is up to you."

Kyle turned to signal to the waiter. The man had

halted just short of their table. Moving uncertainly, he set the entrées in front of them and quickly disappeared.

"Do with it?" Abby looked down at her pasta. It looked, she had to admit, even better than it had sounded. Her stomach rumbled a greeting, reminding her how empty it was, despite her having eaten the roll. Without thinking, she pressed her fingers to her abdomen. "How many options do I have open to me?"

"You can walk away from it, ask the waiter to put it into a take-out box for you. Or—" he leaned forward, his eyes holding her prisoner "—you can have it here, sitting opposite me. The choice is yours."

Her mouth was inexplicably dry. Abby had no doubt that Kyle McDermott was something to see in a business negotiation. He could sure turn up the temperature in a room a degree or two. Or five.

Taking a breath, she sat back in her chair, settling in.

"Well, it's been a while since I've been out to dinner," she said. "Actually," she confessed, "other than family get-togethers, dinner for me is usually something I pick up on the way home, or in the cafeteria at the clinic as I wait out a particularly difficult labor."

He could remember all the times he'd gone hungry, promising himself that there would be a time in his life when he would never want for the essentials again. "You're going about it all wrong."

Curious, Abby raised an eyebrow, waiting to see what wisdom Marcie McDermott's brother was going to share with her now. "Oh?"

"Dinner is something to be savored, not gotten on the run." Which he proceeded to do with the piece of prime rib he had ordered. He'd eaten in the best restaurants and had sampled all sorts of cuisine, but in his heart, he still loved a simple serving of prime rib best.

Abby couldn't have explained why watching him slip the piece of meat between his lips caused her pulse to accelerate. It had to be the wine, she reasoned. Yes, the wine had to be to blame for the rise in room temperature, as well.

"This from a man who makes a habit of skipping dinners at home in favor of a power dinner at some restaurant, ironing out the newest wrinkles in the company's production schedule?"

The words were different, but he recognized the sentiment. Or actually, the accusation. "You *have* gotten close to Marcie."

Abby liked the young woman. When Marcie had initially come to her for prenatal care, there had been a defensiveness about her. It had taken Abby several visits before she could get Marcie to open up, but it had been worth it.

She smiled at his observation. "I suppose I have."

He couldn't help being grateful to Abby. Marcie needed someone to confide in, and it obviously wasn't going to be him this time around. "If you do that with all your patients, I'm surprised you have anything left of yourself to give." He glanced at her, amusement playing on his lips. "And that it doesn't make you even later than you are."

"My being late this morning had nothing to do with my schedule. It had to do with the family." She wasn't about to go into it any more than that. The sordid details were already on the evening news and would undoubtedly make the morning paper. "As for my being close to all my patients, to a greater or lesser degree, I am." She abhorred assembly-line doctoring. That wasn't what she and the clinic were about. "I don't want to be merely some faceless, emotionless voice of authority—

someone who's there to tell the woman to take vitamins and then stand and catch the baby. I'm interested in my patients' overall health and well-being. That means taking an interest in the total person, not just the condition that brought them to me in the first place.''

He noticed the way she used her fork to punctuate her words. Because it was such a vital component in his own life, Kyle had always admired dedication above a great many other attributes. And the lady appeared to have a growing number of them, he noted appreciatively, taking another sip of his wine.

He found himself wondering about her. What made a woman like Abby Maitland, who could have sat back and done nothing except attend parties and have men lavish her with compliments, choose something as difficult as obstetrics, with its invasive calls in the middle of the night and endless hours of work? If she wanted to be a doctor, there were less taxing ways to go.

''If you believe in total care so much, why aren't you a country doctor?''

There were times she'd asked that of herself, as well, Abby thought, though she had never questioned why she entered medicine in the first place. A doctor was what she had wanted to be for as long as she could remember. ''Maitland Maternity Clinic is a cause that is very close to my mother's heart.''

''And you are close to your mother.'' It wasn't a question.

She met his eyes. ''Yes, I am.''

It didn't occur to her to deny it, or insist on the fact that despite her feelings, she was as independent as they came. She was secure in who she was. It was only in the middle of the night, when the place beside her felt so empty, or when she held a brand-new life in her hands—a life that had been created out of love—that she felt an ache and wondered if there would ever be someone to love her for who she was.

"We all are," she added.

Kyle nodded his head in silent tribute. To his knowledge, there had never been a disparaging thing written about Megan Maitland. Unlike so many people in a position of power, she had no detractors—only admirers. That said a great deal about the lady.

"I hear she's a remarkable woman."

"She is."

He heard the pride in Abby's voice. "I'd like to meet her sometime."

Was that as innocent as it sounded? God, when had she become this suspicious of people? But then, she amended, she knew when. Knew exactly when. When her dreams had shattered after Drew's conniving duplicity had come to light.

"Perhaps you will," Abby said evasively, avoiding his eyes. "Sometime."

He had the feeling that Abby was very protective of her mother. It gave them something in common, for he felt the same way about Marcie. Whether or not his sister wanted protecting was another story.

He contemplated his empty glass and then refilled it. Glancing at hers, he topped it off. He noticed that she didn't demur. What would it be like, he wondered, to hold this woman in his arms and taste the wine on her lips? Would it be as intoxicating as the wine itself, or would he be disappointed?

Something told him that *disappointment* was a word that wouldn't enter the picture.

Dismissing thoughts that had no place here, he picked on something she'd mentioned earlier. "You said you thought Marcie was mature for her age.'' He wanted to know if there was something he was missing, or if Abby was just paying lip service. ''How much maturity does it take to have a baby?''

Abby laughed softly. The sound wound around him like steel beams of sunshine, tightening his chest.

''That wasn't why I said she was mature. Her decision to have the baby while not taking the safe route of having someone take care of her is what I find mature.''

Hadn't she been paying attention? ''She has someone to take care of her. Me.''

He didn't understand, did he? she thought. Men seldom did. ''Forgive me, but it's not quite the same thing. And besides,'' she hurried on before he could interrupt, ''if I know Marcie, she's not going to hang around the old homestead, letting you foot all the bills. She has a very independent streak.''

He laughed shortly. ''Tell me something I don't know.''

Kyle thought of all the arguments he and Marcie had had, arguments that had ended with his sister announcing that she was going to get her own place as soon as she was able to get a job. He always thought she said it to hit him where he'd hurt the most. Marcie knew how much he wanted her to get an education, and how important he believed it was to her future to have that degree before she ventured out into the workforce. More than anything else, he wanted her to avoid the hardships he'd had to endure, working and putting himself through school while taking care of a child. In his case, it had been her. Marcie deserved better, and he was going to see that she got it.

He was off somewhere, Abby thought, seeing the

look in his eyes. She placed her hand on top of his to get his attention. "But she loves you very much."

Kyle restrained the sudden, unexpected desire to take her hand in his. Instead, he wound his fingers over the stem of his glass. "Sure doesn't feel that way sometimes."

This time, her laugh was light. "Funny, she says the same thing about you."

He knew from what Marcie had said that Abby Maitland had earned her respect. But how much had his sister actually shared with this woman? "What else does she say about me?"

There was no hesitation as Abby went down the list of adjectives Marcie had used in describing her brother. For all their problems, Marcie still worshipped him. If she hadn't, Abby would have given him an evasive answer.

"That you're overbearing, used to getting your own way and push yourself too hard," she added. Her smile faded. He had to know this. "She also feels that you're not around that much. Not the way you used to be."

He knew that. Regretted it. But there was no other way. Maybe someday, but not yet. "If I'm not around that much, it's because I'm busy making sure that Marcie won't have to be afraid of waking up tomorrow and finding that we're back to living from hand to mouth."

These were details Marcie hadn't touched on. Abby knew that it was because the girl had been too young to remember. But Kyle hadn't. "Did you? Live that way, I mean."

Her voice seemed to touch him, and he suddenly understood why his sister found Abby so easy to talk to. There was genuine concern in her eyes, in her voice.

He found himself talking about things he seldom held up to the light of day. Things he preferred to forget.

"Yes. For five years, when I sold everything but the shoes off my feet to finance what was to become K & M Telecommunication Systems, there was hardly anything in the hand to bring to the mouth. You wouldn't understand what doing without is, Doctor." He stopped, impatient. He'd said too much, admitted too much. It made his temper short. "I can't keep calling you that—not with the candlelight making you look so beautiful. Do you mind if I call you Abby?"

"No. Go right ahead. If you want." The words fell from her lips like so many tiny grains of sand. Her mouth felt far too dry for her to even swallow. Abby reached for the goblet of water beside her half-filled glass of wine and drank deeply. When she was confident that she could form sentences without having them rasp along her throat, she added, "And I wouldn't be so quick, if I were you, to make the assumption that I don't know anything about doing without."

"Oh?" The Maitlands had been well-off for decades. The two of them were worlds apart. Humor tempered his expression. "And what is it that you've ever done without?"

The honest love of a man, she thought. But she wasn't about to tell him that. For Abby, it seemed the more money she had, the more deprived she felt. The more wary she became. And consequently, the lonelier she was in those precious private moments she had. Private moments that she had no one to share with.

Her expression became unreadable. "Nothing that I would be willing to talk about to a relative stranger, Mr. McDermott."

The thought of remaining a stranger had less and less

appeal for Kyle with each passing moment. It had been a long time since he'd found himself wanting to get to know a woman, really know her. Up until now, his work had seemed too important for these kinds of sidebars. Now he wasn't so sure.

"It's Kyle, remember?" he prompted.

Why the reminder should send a ripple through her like a warm caress made no sense. The man was charismatic, but she wasn't here for charisma; she was here to settle something.

Abby lowered her eyes to her plate and was surprised to discover that she had eaten almost everything. She'd been a great deal hungrier than she'd thought. And a lot more distracted.

"This is good," she murmured.

She obviously liked seafood. He went with that. "If you think that's good, I should take you to this little restaurant I know." He thought of the brick-faced building housed in a neighborhood where the residents frequently looked over their shoulder as they walked. He'd found it by accident and kept returning by design. "The area's run-down and there's no decor to speak of, but the owner isn't the type who cares about outside trappings. He does all his own cooking. People have been known to make long pilgrimages just to sample a taste."

Humor shone in her eyes. "I didn't know you were given to exaggeration."

"I'm not."

His expression was pure innocence. She considered herself forewarned.

"Tell you what, why don't I take you there, say, tomorrow night?"

She shook her head. "Tomorrow night's not good for you."

How did she know what was on his calendar? With all the juggling he did, he wasn't even certain himself at this point. "Excuse me?"

"Bewildered" looked appealing on him, she thought. "The birthing class, remember?"

No, he hadn't. Now that she reminded him, Kyle winced. "It's something I'd just as soon forget. Don't get me wrong, Abby, I'd do anything for Marcie. Anything. But standing there while she…she…" The thought of being present while his sister struggled to bring a new life in the world seemed far too personal for him to intrude into. He shrugged away the image that refused to solidify into words. "Well, it's just not the kind of brother-sister bond I had in mind."

She didn't think it was his blood pressure that was causing that faint pink tinge to creep up his neck. That he could be embarrassed amused her; it made him seem more human. She steepled her fingers before her, leaning toward him. "Things don't always go according to plan—and Marcie wouldn't have chosen you if she didn't think you were right for the job."

The woman executed more twists and turns than a winding road on a dark night. He had a feeling she was not one to surrender easily. That's why he really wanted her on his side—and didn't count himself out just yet. "I bet you were the star of your high school debating team."

"Never had the time for that." That had been R.J.'s forte. "I went in for sports."

"Really?" The thought of a common bond sparked his interest. Now that he thought of it, she did have the body of an athlete. "What kind?"

"Track and field."

Had she been the one to seek him out instead of the other way around, he would immediately have thought that she was fabricating things solely to get on his good side. It had been happening a great deal of late. But since he'd been the one to corner her, he had no choice but to believe she was telling the truth.

Now that he thought of it, she had calves like a runner. And legs that would attract the attention of a dead man. "No kidding. Me, too. In high school. There wasn't much time for it in college."

Not when you're dedicated to conquering the known world, she thought, studying him. She wondered if he could be ruthless when he was after something. Marcie hadn't mentioned it, but then Marcie might not know. "Still run?"

"Whenever I can—which isn't often these days." Not nearly as often as he would like.

Abby retired her knife and fork and reached for the glass of wine he'd topped off for her. She took just a taste to complement the meal.

"Me, too. There's nothing like taking a jog through the city before it's awake yet, before the traffic's had a chance to begin choking off the streets and the noise starts coming from everywhere." It was her favorite time of the day, when possibilities lay fresh and unopened.

Kyle banked down suspicions that struggled to come to the fore. She'd just described, almost to a tee, the way he felt about running. If he didn't know better... But he did.

"I miss doing it on a regular basis," he said. "It helps me clear my head."

It didn't, she noticed, do too badly by his body, either. The man looked incredibly fit, to say the least. She knew of several women who, in her situation, would have been drooling long before now.

Kyle felt as if he were the one being scrutinized instead of the other way around, as he'd intended. "What are you smiling about?"

"Nothing." And then, sensing that if she didn't explain, he would only let his imagination run away with him, she said, "I was wondering how you managed to get that physique sitting behind a desk."

"Isometrics. Actually, it's a very heavy desk." This time, it was his turn to grin. "To be honest, I was wondering the same thing about you." He allowed his eyes to travel over her slowly. "You don't look like any doctor I know."

Abby placed her hand at her neck, certain that color was creeping up her skin, grateful for the dim lighting. "Maybe you don't know enough doctors."

Her offhand comment made him think of his father, of the battery of doctors who'd finally been called in. All too late to do anything for a man who had destroyed his liver and other vital organs in his wanton love affair with the bottle. Clinging to denial, Kyle had dropped out of school for six months to care for his father in an effort to save him, but it had been too late to do anything except wait for the inevitable. And silently hold his father's hand.

"I do."

The finality of his tone aroused her curiosity. At the same time, it told her not to press or ask any more questions. She knew what it felt like to have people pry. Abby kept her question to herself. Everyone was entitled to privacy, even pushy executive types with beautiful green eyes.

Another woman would have asked, he thought. But another woman would not have had firsthand experience at being in the limelight through no fault of her own, other than birth. She would respect his privacy.

He found himself wanting to know more about her, and told himself it was because of Marcie.

"So, you don't think that Marcie should get another coach." The fresh question banished the awkward tension between them.

The hopeful note was hard to miss. Abby shook her head. "No."

"And you don't agree that Marcie should get married before the baby's born."

Was he just recapping, or hoping she would change her mind the second time around? "Not if she doesn't want to." An impish smile played on Abby's lips. She wasn't as tired as she'd initially thought, but she knew the evening had to come to an end. She had a C-section scheduled first thing in the morning and she had to be rested for it.

She glanced to see if her purse was still on the floor, or if she'd accidentally kicked it under the table. "I guess from your point of view, you just wasted some more precious time."

He was losing her attention. It was obvious she was getting ready to leave.

"No," he told her quietly. He saw her look up at him. "I didn't." Kyle leaned forward. "Would you be interested in going to that restaurant I mentioned earlier?" He wanted to take her to Simon's. Wanted to see her reaction. He had a feeling that Dr. Abby Maitland was a woman who was passionate about more things than just her patients and running. "I promise you, you've never had food like this before."

"You've aroused my curiosity," she admitted.

And she, with her trim figure, her fascinating eyes, her quick wit and quicker tongue, had done more than arouse his. For the first time in a long time, Kyle realized that his mind hadn't strayed to his work during the meal. Instead, he found questions forming in his mind about the woman he'd just shared dinner with.

"Good, then since I seem to be booked up tomorrow night, how does the night after that strike you?" She was hesitating, so he took a guess. "Provided I'm not stepping on anyone's toes."

She'd been grilled by people who were better at it than he was. From overbearing big brothers when she was a teenager to snoopy reporters posing as college students. It gave her a sixth sense about these things, about questions that were really more than they seemed.

"Are you asking me if I'm involved with someone?"

He was slipping, Kyle thought, but it had been a long time since he'd asked a woman out just for her company. "Not quite so bluntly, but yes, I am."

"I'm not." It occurred to her that the words seemed to just hang in the air. "Involved with anyone," she added.

If asked, he wouldn't have been able to explain why that information pleased him the way it did. He had no grand plan involving Abby. He would have balked at one, had it been suggested.

"Neither am I."

"Marcie says you are."

His brow furrowed. He and Marcie didn't spend as much time together as he would like, especially now that Billy had entered her life and the possibility of the company going public had entered his. But he would have told his sister if there was someone special. And he hadn't. Why would Marcie think there was?

"Who?"

"Not who—what," Abby corrected, and her meaning immediately dawned on him. "Marcie says that your company has a firmer grip on you than if it were a conniving woman. I'd say that tells a lot about how Marcie feels about your work."

They'd been through this before, he and Marcie. "Like it's competition."

Abby nodded. "Like it's competition."

"That's ridiculous," Kyle said, summarily dismissing the idea.

But Abby wasn't as ready as he was to give the notion a final send-off. "Is it? I'd think about it if I were you. You said you'd be willing to give her anything she wanted. I think all she wants is you. That's why she asked you to be her coach. She wants to be part of your life again before you both go your separate ways, living very separate lives."

For that, he didn't have to be subjected to birthing films that threatened to separate him from his last meal, did he? "She always has been part of my life."

He believed that, she thought. And maybe, from his point of view, it was true. But there was another point of view to take into consideration. "Maybe it's time you let her know. Sit down, talk with her."

"Hasn't Marcie told you how many times I've tried to talk to her?"

"*To* her, *at* her." Abby paused. "What you need to do is talk *with* her. A dialogue, not a monologue or a lecture. Find out what she's feeling. Your sister might act tough, but she's a scared little girl under all that."

He thought he'd caught her in a contradiction. "I thought you said she was mature."

"She hasn't let you see that scared little girl, has she?"

As slippery as an eel and as desirable as a legendary mermaid. "Did you minor in psychology?"

"No, in brothers and sisters." She placed her napkin on the table. "I put in a lot of hours of observation when I was growing up." Abby rose. "Thank you for dinner, Kyle. Sorry I couldn't have been more persuadable. Or persuasive. But now I really have to be going."

He knew roughly what the check would come to. He added twenty percent and left the bills on the table. Not about to let her get away, he was beside her before she took more than a few steps. "About that restaurant?"

He knew how to wear someone down, Abby thought. She supposed there was no harm in accepting. She did love lobster. "If there's no emergency…"

"Goes without saying."

"All right," she said, wondering why it felt as if she were about to take that first step down from the shuttle onto the surface of the moon. "You can pick me up at eight."

"Seven might be better."

He probably wanted to get in a late meeting after dinner, she mused. "All right, seven then."

She wasn't quite sure what to make of the smile that came to his face, but she had a feeling she was going to have to be on her guard, the next time they met.

CHAPTER SIX

THE STAGNANT AIR within the motel room threatened to choke her. The smell of stale cigarettes and cheap perfume clung to the threadbare curtains and stained bedspread, held there by dust that had long since turned to grit. It was too cold to open a window, too stifling to keep it shut.

She felt like a caged animal.

Any second now, Janelle thought, she was going to crawl out of her own skin. Impatience tightened around her like a vise as she paced the small enclosure, one hand wrapped around the faintly sticky telephone receiver, the other around a chunky glass filled with amber liquid. An opened bottle stood on the chipped dresser.

On the other end of the line, Petey was giving her a hard time. As if she didn't have enough to deal with. That's what she got for throwing her lot in with a spineless weasel. He was gorgeous to look at, but utterly lacking as far as brains went.

She had half a mind to cut him loose and throw him the hell out of her life. The attraction that had drawn them together in Vegas had faded for her faster than the wedding vows they'd exchanged.

But though she hated the fact, she needed him. She couldn't pull this colossal deception off on her own. Megan Maitland had given birth all those years back to a son, not a daughter. It was too late to bring someone else into this. Besides, there was no way in hell she was going to trust yet another person with the details. It was bad enough she'd had to trust Petey. A secret shared was a secret that could turn on you and destroy everything.

She wasn't about to take that chance. She was already trying to deal with one unforeseen twist; she couldn't handle any more. Losing Lacy's baby like that had been a major setback—one she was still trying to turn to her advantage.

In the background, the program on one of the all-news cable stations was replaying itself to the empty double bed. The words were only half registering. Janelle had heard it all before, several times. It was the only thing that had given her hope. The drama, she thought with a smile, was appropriately heightening.

Now all she needed was to get that sorry-assed, cow-chips-for-brains husband of hers to work with her on this. "Don't give me any grief, Petey," she warned before taking another deep gulp of the whiskey she clutched. Some of it dribbled onto her chin. She used the side of her hand to wipe it away, then ran her tongue over the moist area. Waste not, want not, right? "I'm the one doing most of the work here. If you don't get that tattoo, the whole damn thing falls apart on us."

She heard his anger resonating over the line. Petey had to be drinking. He would never have raised his voice to her otherwise. "I said I don't want anyone sticking any damn needles into me. Why can't I be the kid's father without a damn tattoo?"

"Because it's supposed to be a hereditary birthmark, you freakin' idiot." How many times did she have to explain this to him? "You have to have it, too, like the baby, so there's no way any of the Maitlands're going to doubt that you're the father of the kid. Connor O'Hara, remember? Their long-lost cousin and the high-and-mighty Megan Maitland's not-so-dead son come to life. Damn it, Petey, just how stupid are you?''

She heard the sharp intake of breath and knew that she'd pushed him too far. "At least I'm not stupid enough to lose the kid in the first place.''

Janelle struggled with her anger. Once this was over, she'd find a way to be rid of him for good. "I already told you, Lacy put him down on the steps when I lunged at her. When I came out of the alley, there were all these reporters around him. How was I to know the Maitlands were going to hold a damn press conference?'' She took another long swallow; it only fueled her anger. "I couldn't get close—not without blowing everything. I've worked too hard to have that happen now.'' She blew out a ragged breath, trying to control her temper. Yelling at him was pointless. She needed him on her side, not blocking her every move.

"Look, I'm sorry. It's just that I've been flipping around all the channels and nobody's said nothing about finding a body in that alley.''

She'd left Lacy bloodied and still behind a Dumpster, certain that she was dead. Relieved that she was dead. All those months of pretending to be Lacy's friend just to get her hands on the baby—success had all been within her reach. Now the certainty was deserting her. Possible scenarios began forming in Janelle's head, all ending with the slam of a cell door.

"What if Lacy's not dead? What if she goes to the police—?'' Janelle could hear the panic in her own voice.

"They would have said that, too.'' A note akin to

compassion came into Petey's voice. He was a prisoner of his own greed and his own libido, and Janelle could satisfy his lust like no one else. Added to that, she had a head on her shoulders that was as larcenous as his. It was a match made in hell and it suited him just fine. "Take it easy, Janelle, maybe they just haven't found her yet."

Draining the last of the whiskey, she set the glass down beside the bottle. The breath she let out was shaky. She clutched at the excuse Petey gave her. "Yeah, you're probably right. I'm worrying for nothing."

She looked back at the set and saw a fuzzy shot of the baby she had kidnapped. The one she meant to pass off as her own. Time was running out. "But we still have to work fast before something else comes up." She purposely softened her voice. "Okay, will you do it, Petey? Please? It's just a small, crescent-shaped tattoo. I can fax a drawing of it to you. What's a little tattoo to a big, strong guy like you? Think of what's at stake. All that money…"

He muttered a ripe curse. The woman would keep at it until he gave in. He thought of his sister. Roz was a makeup artist for some big studio out west. An idea came to him, and then his lips twitched in a half smile. "Okay, okay, I'll do it. Send me the fax."

Now that she had her way, Janelle could afford to be nice. "I knew I could count on you, darlin'. It'll be worth it, just wait and see. We're going to be rich, Petey—richer than you ever thought possible."

She heard the deep chuckle in her ear. "Nobody's got *that* kind of money. Not even God."

Maybe, she thought, but the Maitlands came close.

BONE WEARY, KYLE drew his key out of the lock. All he wanted to do right now was fall facedown on his bed. He'd worry about changing out of his clothes later. Like tomorrow. The suit was supposed to resist wrinkles. Now would be a good time to test it.

"So, how did it go?"

Startled, he pivoted on his heel to see that Marcie was in the living room. She'd turned her chair so that she faced the front door like a sentry. She'd obviously been waiting up for him. From the cluster of empty candy wrappers around the chair, she'd been waiting for some time.

She rolled the last wrapper between her thumb and forefinger before dropping it. "Looks like you put in a little overtime with my doctor."

He was still tired, but he was also alert now. "Dinner was over a while ago. She went home, I stopped by the office."

"Surprise, surprise." Using her knuckles, Marcie awkwardly dug herself out of her chair. She crossed to him, each step labored. "Since you didn't score, you could have come home."

He knew she talked like that just to irritate him. "I didn't try to 'score.' And I didn't think I'd find anyone to come home to. I thought you'd be with Billy." The few occasions he'd had a little time to spare, Marcie had been off somewhere with her boyfriend.

The corners of her mouth turned down. Though her voice was hard, sarcastic, Kyle thought he saw the shimmer of tears in her eyes. "Billy's parents think he shouldn't see me for a while."

Billy's parents were afraid that Kyle would take them to court to get them to pay for expenses, Kyle thought. The two times he'd tried to get in contact with them, they had been completely uncooperative. "Too bad they didn't think that way eight months ago."

Marcie's chin shot up, fury in her eyes. "A lot you care."

The recrimination stopped him short. He caught her by the shoulders, holding her fast. "I care, Marcie. I care a lot."

Her anger only grew. "Is that why you're trying to turn Abby against me?"

Is that what she thought? How had they managed to get so far apart? Weary, he dropped his hands from her shoulders. "Nobody's turning against you, Marcie. I just thought that if someone you liked tried to talk some sense into you, you'd listen."

Marcie resented the way Kyle treated her like a child, instead of as a full-grown woman who was about to have her own baby. She'd expected better of her brother. "When I hear sense, I will."

Kyle struggled to hang on to his temper. Losing it hadn't done anything except drive them further apart. "She thinks we should talk."

They never talked anymore, Marcie thought. All they did was yell. She was as guilty as he was. Maybe guiltier. But she wouldn't be, if only he were as understanding as he used to be when she was younger. When he'd sat by her bed whenever she had nightmares, reading to her until she fell asleep again. Talking to her about his dreams for the future.

"Did you tell her you yell at me?"

"I don't yell—" He heard his voice rising and held it in check. "I get a little vocal when you tune me out, that's all." He took Marcie's hands in his, turning her so that she had to look up at him. "Marcie, what's wrong with getting married? You told me you love him.''

''I did and I do.'' They'd been through this already. Why couldn't he understand? He was supposed to be the older one—the one with more experience. Why was it that she inherently knew this and he didn't? ''But love falls apart if there're too many demands put on it. Billy's not ready to be a husband yet, or a full-time father. He needs to grow up.'' She pulled her hands free and backed away, feeling desperate. ''I wish you'd understand, Kyle.''

But he wasn't about to give up. ''And I wish *you'd* understand that despite great strides the world's still a hard place for a single mother with a child. They won't stone you, but—'' Words deserted him. They always did when it was something important like this; something in which his heart took precedence over his mind. ''I want you to have all the advantages I didn't.''

Why was he so hung up on this? Marriage was just an archaic symbol of a long-ago time. ''I think Mom would have been better off if she'd opted not to marry Dad when she found out she was pregnant with you. She would have been happier. We all would have.''

Kyle stared at her. It seemed to him that he had always known about his parents' hasty marriage, but he'd thought that Marcie had been kept in the dark. He had never mentioned it himself.

''How did you know?''

He really did think she was a child, Marcie thought. Resentment built. ''I've known for a long time. It was during one of their arguments before Mom died.'' She shrugged carelessly. ''Kids hear things.'' Especially when ''things''—accusations about entrapment—were being shouted across a room.

She was never going to hear Billy say that to her.

Kyle had been through this too many times to think that they were going to resolve anything or make some sort of breakthrough tonight. They would only go round and round the same worn path. Turning away from her, he headed for the stairs.

"I'm too tired to have this argument again now, Marcie. I'm going to bed. I'd advise you to do the same. Pretend it's someone else telling you."

With that, he started to walk up the stairs.

"So, am I going to get a lecture next time I go in for a checkup?" Marcie called after him.

"No." He glanced back at her. "She thinks you should do what you want."

Marcie grinned triumphantly. "You could learn a couple of things from Dr. Maitland."

Kyle headed back up the stairs, his own lips curving in a smile. It didn't sound like that bad an idea to him. But not for the reasons Marcie thought.

IT HAD BEEN A LONG TIME since Megan had felt this restless. No matter which way she had turned, or how much she had plumped her pillow last night, sleep had refused to come.

Ever since she'd taken the baby into her arms yesterday, she had found herself in a heightened state of agitation. Oh, not so that anyone around her would actually take notice. Externally, she remained calm. She had become too well-groomed in the ways of her world not to. With all eyes on her, Megan had gone about her business, had taken steps to push forward an investigation she could control herself.

But inside, inside where that awkward, shy young

woman, Megan Kelly, resided, it was a different story. There the restlessness took root.

There was something about that infant, something she couldn't put her finger on. A feeling that passed over her when she held him. She couldn't really describe it; she could only feel it.

As if there truly was a bond between them.

She couldn't know that for sure. All she had was a piece of paper that could very well be a hoax—a publicity stunt that made shameless use of an innocent child. That and a tiny bracelet with the initials *CO*. Initials that could mean anything, belong to anyone.

But there was that feeling…

Megan repositioned her grip on the steering wheel.

She was becoming a silly old woman before her time. Otherwise, why wasn't she still in bed instead of driving to Maitland Maternity at this hour?

Was she going there to assure herself that she hadn't imagined it all?

If she had, hundreds of people had hallucinated right along with her. That was how many people must have seen Chelsea Markum's show. Not to mention the news.

"Is the abandoned baby the result of a fling on the part of one of the Maitland men?" The teaser had been voiced by eager newscaster after newscaster, deftly slipped in right before the local weather or sports.

"Please stand by and find out."

Except that there was nothing to find out. Yet.

Leaving her car parked in her reserved space at the front of the lot, Megan made her way into the building. She pushed open the door and walked down the long, bright hallway, past the sleeping gift shop, and the day care center, heading toward the nursery. Megan nodded at the security guard. The older man looked a little surprised to see her.

That makes two of us, she thought.

Her own first baby had been born in the winter. Nine months after Clyde Maitland Mitchum had promised to love her forever. Six months after he'd permanently disappeared from her life, fleeing the responsibility of having to care for a seventeen-year-old girl and their bastard child.

She had never heard from him again. Her father had told her later that Clyde had been killed in a freak riding accident.

At the time, she had felt empty. But her tears had been for the baby who had never had a chance to live. Now, with all her heart, she wished she could have held that baby in her arms just once. Her firstborn. Stillborn. Like Clyde's love.

The hallway divided. Megan automatically turned right, walking by the labor, delivery and recovery rooms. The clinic boasted ten each. They were all a blur to her. Why was she dwelling on this now, after so many years? Granted, the ache of losing her son had never fully left her, but it wasn't something she thought about often these days.

Not the way she'd done forty-five years ago.

But holding that baby yesterday had somehow aroused all those dormant thoughts, touched off memories that had been so long sealed away....

Megan shook off her mood and walked softly into the nursery.

There was a nurse tending to a newborn on the far side of the room. She looked up when Megan entered.

"Ma'am, you can't—'' And then recognition set in. "Mrs. Maitland. Oh, I'm sorry, I didn't realize it was you.'' Tucking the baby against her, the nurse came forward. ''Is there something I can do for you?'' Her eyes strayed toward the large clock on the back wall.

The woman probably thought she was crazy, Megan surmised. Maybe she was, but she had needed to come here. Had felt compelled to come. ''No, I just wanted to see how the baby was doing.''

There was one bassinet separated from all the others. It was as if it belonged to a pariah. Megan knew without being told that the foundling was in it. Wordlessly, she went to him.

''He's doing fine.'' The nurse followed her. ''Hasn't fussed since I came on.''

As if to disprove her, the baby began to cry.

''Until now,'' she said with a laugh. ''I'll just put this little guy down and—''

But Megan waved her back. ''That's all right, I'll tend to him. You already have your hands full.'' She saw the quizzical look on the younger woman's face. ''I don't mind, really.''

Picking the infant up, Megan sighed softly as she brought the baby to her. She could feel her heart swelling as she laid her cheek against him. ''Who are you, little one, and what are you doing here?''

Only a cry answered her question.

She looked down at him and smiled. ''Well, we'll put those questions on hold for the time being and turn our attention to a more immediate problem. You need to be changed, young man.'' Still holding the baby, Megan turned toward the nurse. ''Julie, where do we keep the diapers? This little fella needs changing.''

''Right here.'' Her arms free again, the nurse hurried over to the closet where the supplies were kept. She opened the double doors and quickly removed what was needed then, and walked back to Megan. "I can—"

Megan took the diaper from her and set it on the side, then accepted the powder and wipes. "Yes, I'm sure you can, but I want to. Really," she assured Julie. Placing the baby back in the bassinet, she felt fond memories flood her. "I changed the diapers of every one of my children, even though William kept insisting we had a nanny for that." She pulled out several wipes and placed them beside the clean diaper, at the ready. "I always wanted to do it myself. I didn't have children so that other women could tend to them." She murmured the last more to herself and to the baby than to the nurse. The baby grimaced, his legs kicking. "Hold still," she instructed softly, and pulled off the two tabs. "I promise this isn't going to hurt a bit."

Megan's heart felt as if it had stopped beating.

There, exposed by the diaper she'd just peeled back, was a small crescent-shaped birthmark just above his navel.

The room felt as if it were spinning. Megan gripped the sides of the bassinet, drawing air in slowly until she could focus again. She blinked and looked again. It wasn't her imagination. The vivid outline was still there.

A chill shimmied up and down her spine.

She'd seen a birthmark like that only once before. On Clyde. He'd had one in exactly the same place. His had been almost faint in comparison, or maybe that was just her memory.

Megan could remember tracing it with the tip of her finger, thrilling to the way Clyde's stomach tightened when she touched his skin. When she'd remarked on the birthmark in innocent curiosity, he'd told her that his mother's father had had one, too. To Clyde, the birthmark was equal to the mark of Cain, branding him a Maitland, and he hated it. But then, Clyde had hated the Maitlands, too. As a distant cousin, he'd resented that they were rich and he was not. Every effort William's father had made to reach out to him, Clyde had turned into something ugly.

Looking back, she realized how full of hate he'd actually been.

When her own babies were born, she'd checked each one carefully, looking for the birthmark, afraid of finding it. Afraid any child who had it might be like Clyde in temperament. But none of the children had had the mark. Nor had William. After a while, she'd decided that the whole story had been just a one of Clyde's silly fabrications.

Until now.

Slowly, her breath returned, filling her lungs again. Her pulse steadied. "You really are a Maitland," she whispered.

"Mother, what are you doing here?"

Like a rush of warm sunshine, Abby's voice surrounded her. Turning, Megan saw her daughter walking toward her.

"Taking inventory," Megan quipped. Coming to life, she quickly wiped the small bottom and deftly began diapering the baby. The diaper was on, the crescent safely hidden, before Abby reached her side. "And seeing if I still had what it takes to change a diaper." Finishing up, she folded the dirty diaper and tossed it into the wastebasket. "More important, what is my finest obstetrician doing here?"

"Mary Healy decided she wanted a baby in September instead of October."

The call had come in from the answering service

shortly after ten o'clock last night. It was just as well. Abby had had a feeling that she wasn't going to get much sleep, anyway. Kyle McDermott kept invading her thoughts, throwing her off-kilter. She wasn't quite sure how she felt about him. Or how she wanted to feel.

Hand pressed to the small of her back, she rotated her shoulders and tried to vanquish the ache that was lingering there. She'd spent the last hour, it seemed, bent over the howling Mary. Thank God, the woman hadn't had triplets. Otherwise, Abby felt her hearing might never be the same again.

"It was a long labor. I wish these babies were more cooperative."

Tucking the blanket around the baby, Megan picked him up and cuddled him against her shoulder. She smiled knowingly at Abby. "That's right, you had a late night, didn't you?"

Abby lifted a shoulder indifferently, then let it drop. "Not so late."

Megan regarded her daughter with interest, wondering if Abby was being deliberately vague. She'd been so different before, when she was seeing Drew. More carefree, happier. When they broke up, the light had left her eyes for a long time.

"How did your evening go?"

Abby looked at the sea of tiny faces, so many of whom she'd delivered. The numbers never really penetrated until she saw them together like this. A lot of new little citizens had come into the world this last week, she mused.

"It went."

Megan read between the lines. "In other words, don't pry." She accepted the silent command with the grace that was her hallmark.

Abby sank her hands into her pockets. What was Kyle doing right now? she wondered suddenly. She glanced at the back clock. Probably sleeping like every other normal person.

"Pry all you want, Mother, there's nothing to tell. I had dinner with Kyle McDermott, and he tried to talk me into backing him up with his sister. He failed." *And sometime during the evening, without so much as a single warning, he managed to slip himself into the recesses of my mind.*

She had to get out more, she told herself.

With a touch of reluctance, Megan placed the baby back in his bassinet. Then she slipped an arm around Abby's shoulders and gave her daughter an affectionate hug. "I don't find that surprising. No one could ever make you do anything unless you wanted to. You were always my stubborn little warrior."

"Speaking of warriors—" Abby nodded toward the bassinet and its occupant "—do you think he's really a Maitland?"

The smile on Megan's face grew serious. "I'm sure of it."

Her mother said it with such conviction, there seemed to be no room for doubt. "Why?"

Megan wanted to tell her, but there was so much to share and now just didn't seem the appropriate time. "For the moment, Abby, you're simply going to have to trust me and take my word for it."

Abby cocked her head, studying her mother's face. Her mother really *was* serious. "You're being very mysterious, Mother."

"Mysterious" made it sound as if she were playing

games, Megan thought. But there were reasons for what she was doing. Good ones. Megan chose her words carefully. "Let's just say, I'm being cautious."

"Okay," Abby agreed gamely, "let's."

CHAPTER SEVEN

"OKAY, SO WHAT'S THIS about you and the gorgeous hunk?"

Dana ambushed Abby with the question even before she had a chance to put her tray down on the table.

Abby's friends Katie Topper and Hope Logan, the owner of the gift shop on the clinic's premises, were already seated on either side of Dana. The last space belonged to Abby.

Friends from early childhood, the four had made a pact just after Abby and Hope, who were three years older than Dana and Katie, had graduated from high school. It was a simple pact with one requirement: remain in touch. Part of that pact included having lunch together at least once a week whenever possible. Since they now all worked at the same facility, the effort didn't require as much maneuvering as it had when they'd been attending three different colleges. But with Abby's busy schedule, it wasn't always easy, either.

Normally, lunch with "the girls" was something Abby looked forward to. But she wasn't sure about today. She had a feeling she was in for a triple dose of the third degree.

Looking at Dana, her brother's executive secretary, Abby tried to sound as casual as she could. Word seemed to travel faster within the infrastructure of Maitland Maternity than it might even in a small town.

"You tell me, Dana, since you seem to know more than I do."

Hope looked a little disappointed. "Then you *didn't* go out with Kyle McDermott, the new darling of the computer world?"

Now that her own marriage to Drake was in temporary limbo, Hope welcomed the diversion of a little excitement in her friend's social life, even if short-lived. Until this morning, they had all but given up on the idea that Abby would ever *have* a social life again. Of the four of them, Abby was the only one whose life was not linked, at least in some form or another, to a man's. Katie was secretly in love with Ford Carrington, Maitland's pediatric surgeon, and Dana—well, Dana had been crazy about her boss, R.J., for what seemed like forever. And Hope, of course, was waiting for Drake to come to his senses.

Katie moved her tray back, giving Abby more room.

"No, I didn't." Abby sat down, then reconsidered the firm denial. "At least, not exactly."

Dana looked at her, amused. They should have expected as much. Abby was very guarded when it came to her personal life, even with her closest friends. "Just how does one go out with Kyle McDermott 'not exactly'? Either you do or you don't." She glanced at the others, suppressing a smile. "Seems pretty straightforward to me."

"If I'd been out with him last night, I'd sure know it." Katie sighed with more than a little feeling. Dana had pulled up a photograph of the man on the internet and printed it out for all of them to look at. Katie took a sip of her coffee. "You know, it's hard to believe that something that handsome actually has a functioning brain."

"More than functioning," Dana interjected. She had read the article that accompanied the photograph and had come away impressed not only with Kyle McDermott's creativity, but his business acumen, as well. "According to the business section, Kyle McDermott is the sole power behind K & M Telecommunication Systems."

Hope frowned. "Then who's the *M* supposed to be?"

The answer fell into place for Abby. "That would probably be his sister, Marcie." It made perfect sense, and now that she thought of it, it was rather sweet. It also appeared to be typical of what she'd learned of the man last night. "He named it after her as a symbol of the bond between them, I guess."

Katie leaned back in her seat, pleased that the rumor had turned out to be true. They'd all been worried about Abby after she'd broken up with Drew. She'd practically become a nun.

"So, you did go out with him." Katie's eyes sparkled. "Okay, we're all ears. Tell us everything."

Abby turned her attention to her lunch. Like everything else that had to do with Maitland Maternity, the cafeteria food was above average, but her appetite seemed to have deserted her. "Nothing to tell, really." Sensing Katie was going to prod her further, Abby raised her eyes and looked at her friends, "I didn't go out with him the way you mean. He just wanted to talk."

Dana saw no problem with that. "Talk is good."

"Talk leads to other things," Katie teased. She leaned closer to Abby. "Oh, please, tell me it led to other things. I need a little inspiration in my life."

They were all so close that Abby knew exactly what Katie was referring to. She seized the momentary respite. "Things still not going anywhere between you and Ford?"

Katie gave an exasperated huff. The respected pediatric surgeon seemed to attract glamorous fashion models and literally had his pick of them. There was no way she could hope to compete with that. Dabbling with the dissolving foam on her cappuccino, she shrugged listlessly. "He thinks I'm a bang-up nurse. I'm not even sure he knows I'm female."

Katie had always underestimated both her features and her skills. "Oh, I'm sure he knows," Abby assured her. "I—"

"You're avoiding the issue at hand, Abby," Dana cut in. "We all know you too well. This is called diversion."

"This is called interest in my friend," Abby corrected tersely. "Besides, I don't have anything to tell you about last night."

Dana looked at her knowingly. "That good, huh?"

"That empty." With a sigh, Abby leaned forward over her tray, ignoring the half of a sandwich she had left. "Okay, here's all I can tell you. His sister is a patient of mine. The two of them have a difference of opinion regarding Marcie's future plans, and he asked me out to convince me to try to sway his sister to his way of thinking."

"Why doesn't he try talking to her himself?" Dana asked.

"I hear he's got a golden tongue," Hope added.

More like one made out of lead, Abby thought.

Katie thought of the photograph Dana had pulled up on the internet. "He could certainly talk *me* into something—or out of it." Katie's eyes took on a wicked gleam. "The man is to die for."

Abby, Hope noted, wasn't talking. Getting her to say anything was like pulling teeth. Perhaps there was something to this, after all. Hope asked her next question with barely subdued relish. "So how did all this convincing wind up with your having dinner at Le Vin Rose?"

Abby's mouth dropped open. That was more than an educated guess or speculative rumor. "How do you know that?"

Hope suppressed a laugh. It wasn't easy taking Abby by surprise. She was usually unflappable. "A friend of mine is a waiter there. He mentioned it to Drake, who passed it on."

Abby's surprise melted into a smile. She exchanged looks with the others. "Are you and Drake talking?"

"Civilly." Hope shook her head. "You're doing it again. Diverting attention from yourself."

"No, really, Hope, there's nothing to tell any of you. Really." Abby crossed her heart solemnly, the way they had when they were little. She deliberately banked down the memory of the electricity she'd felt when her hand had accidentally touched Kyle's. Besides, it meant nothing. "I told him his sister was capable of making her own decisions, and I wasn't getting involved."

Dana sighed. "So you're not going to see him again?"

Abby's mind strayed to the invitation Kyle had extended. She pressed her lips together, debating whether to say anything. Not to would be a sin of omission, and they'd call her on it if any of them found out. "Well, as a matter of fact—"

Katie stopped pushing coleslaw around on her plate and came back to life. "Aha!"

Abby held up a hand before Katie could get off and running. "We both like seafood," she explained calmly, though admittedly her inward reaction was not quite so calm—but again, that was too silly to talk about. They were all grown women, for heaven's sake. "He mentioned knowing a restaurant I might like, then suggested taking me there. No big deal."

Obviously, that wasn't the way her friends saw it.

Katie grinned. "Talking, eating—I call that real progress." She leaned her chin on her upturned hand and gazed up at Abby, fluttering her lashes. "So, what'll your firstborn be called?"

Abby popped a French fry into her mouth. "How about Snoopy, after my best friends?"

Hope laughed. "Works for me."

Abby rolled her eyes. There was no stopping them once they got going. "You are hopeless, all of you."

"Oh no, ever hopeful, Abby," Hope told her with mock solemnity. "Ever hopeful."

A sudden beeping noise brought an abrupt halt to the conversation and had all of them looking down at their pagers.

"It's mine," Abby announced, seeing a familiar number register on the small LCD screen.

"Maybe that's Kyle," Dana suggested, struggling to keep a straight face, "calling to find out what you'll be wearing."

Katie grinned. "Tell him plastic wrap, and there's a prize in it for him if he can peel it off you in under five minutes."

Shaking her head, Abby rose. "For your information, it's my mother's office paging me."

The remaining three groaned in unison.

"Better luck next time," Hope called after her, as Abby began her quest for an unoccupied telephone.

Apparently the only secret going undetected here, Abby thought as she crossed the busy room, was the identity of the mother of the abandoned baby. The longer that went unanswered, the bigger the field day the press was going to have. She had a feeling that the worst was yet to come.

The nearest free phone turned out to be at the other end of the dining hall. Picking up the receiver, Abby dialed her mother's extension. "Hi, Mother, it's Abby. You paged me?"

"Yes, I did. The woman from Social Services just called. She's on her way over." This was even faster than they'd anticipated. "I'd like you with me when she comes, if you don't mind. Can you find someone to cover your patients for you?"

Abby was aware how personal this issue had become to her mother. How could she possibly say no?

"I'll be right there, Mother," she promised.

"Thank you, Abby. I appreciate your support."

LEAVING HER DESSERT to be split among her three friends, Abby carried her tray to the conveyor belt, with Katie's instruction to "Keep us posted" following her retreat. She waved a dismissive hand at them, not bothering to look back.

Hurrying from the cafeteria, she went to the elevators. Her mother's words came echoing back to her. *I appreciate your support.*

Abby couldn't help feeling flattered. After all this time, her mother was finally leaning on her, if only a tiny bit. Ever since she was a little girl, she'd watched and admired her mother as she went through life—a strong, independent woman making a place for herself, accomplishing great things even when the odds were against her. Megan Kelly Maitland made a wonderful role model.

But there were times—selfish times, Abby would be the first to admit—when she had longed to be consulted. It wasn't hard to feel superfluous in her mother's world, though she was sure her mother would be appalled if she knew that sort of message was being conveyed.

I appreciate your support.

Abby smiled to herself. It was nice to finally be thought of as an equal.

It occurred to her, as she stepped off the elevator, that it wouldn't hurt Kyle McDermott to be made aware that a similar need was undoubtedly flowering within Marcie. He'd told her that he had taken care of his sister for the past ten years. Abby had no doubt that he had. But that was also the trouble. Marcie didn't strike her as the kind of young woman who wanted to be taken care of twenty-four hours a day. Marcie was like Abby. She wanted to be consulted about what went on in her own life.

More important, she wanted to make the decisions, not have them made for her, even by a loving brother. She wanted to be treated as his equal.

Abby made a mental note to bring this up to Kyle the next time she saw him.

The next time.

Butterflies unaccountably rose in her stomach, fluttering their wings fast enough to have caused a minor hurricane had they been real instead of imaginary. She pressed her hand to her abdomen. Now what was *that* all about? It had to be the conversation she'd just had with Katie, Hope and Dana. That, and maybe too much oil on her French fries. The cafeteria tended to be a little heavy-handed when it came to deep-frying.

For now, she pushed all thoughts of Kyle McDermott, his sister and the pending invitation out of her head. Her mother needed her.

Needed.

It had a very nice ring to it.

HER FINGERS SLIPPERY, Abby dropped the decorative hair clip on the rug for the third time. Stooping down to pick it up, she muttered under her breath, "Thank God you're not that much of a butterfingers with babies or else you'd be out of obstetrics for good. What the hell's the matter with you?"

There was absolutely no reason to feel nervous. She was just going out for a simple dinner in what sounded like a run-down area. Which meant that she was probably overdressed in the ice-blue sheath she had finally decided on after pulling almost everything she owned from her closet. No matter what she'd tried on, nothing had seemed quite right.

Neither did this, Abby thought, slowly turning around and looking herself over in the mirrored wardrobe door.

Too late to change now.

She sighed. Her friends were to blame for this, she thought. If they hadn't made her focus on how good-looking Kyle was at lunch yesterday, how smart and what a catch he was, she wouldn't be behaving like a pubescent on the verge of her first—

Abruptly, Abby stopped fussing with her hair. Her first *what?* First date? First prom? First night of hot, passionate lovemaking?

Her hand fell to her side as she stared at her reflection. Where had that come from?

"Damn it, Katie," she said aloud. "I was fine until you, Hope and Dana started carrying on about him, planting these ideas in my head."

Maybe this wasn't such a good idea, after all. She wasn't accustomed to going out in the middle of the week. There was too much to tend to, and she had all those patients to see tomorrow. Maybe—

The doorbell rang.

The knot in her stomach tightened. Too late to bail out, she thought. Taking the kind of deep, cleansing breath she always counseled about-to-be-mothers to take, she filled her lungs and then slowly let it out. Done correctly, this was supposed to make her feel calmer, more in control.

It didn't.

"This is ridiculous—I'm a grown woman." A grown woman, she reminded herself silently, without all that much experience. She hadn't given her heart easily. Drew had been her first and last lover.

And her first and last fiasco.

"You're not going to make another mistake, you hear?" she ordered herself. Squaring her shoulders, she went to open the door and greet him.

SHE'D BEEN ON HIS MIND since he'd left her in the parking lot the night before last. Not just because he wanted to convince her to side with him. As it stood right now, that was pretty much a dead issue.

No, she'd been haunting him like a lyric he couldn't quite shake free of, and he realized there were things he wanted to do with her other than carry on a debate. Things that had no connection to his sister.

He wanted to know what it felt like to hold Abby Maitland in his arms. What it felt like to kiss the smile from her face and absorb it into his system. It had nothing to do with the fact she was a Maitland and represented some last, lingering fantasy from his too-long-ago youth. It was Abby the woman who intrigued him. The woman who had somehow found her way into his subconscious and stirred him.

There was no other reason for him to be here, standing before the door of her stucco and adobe, western-style house. Lord knew, he had enough things demanding his attention even at this moment. There were a hundred things he could be doing rather than ringing her doorbell.

None of them remotely tempted him.

For the first time in a long while, Kyle was allowing himself a respite. An interlude of promised pleasure, or, at the very least, a real break in his routine and the treadmill his life had become.

She opened the door, looking a little breathless. Looking, he thought, like the stuff that fantasies were made of.

"Wow."

Was he teasing her, or on the level? Abby wondered. And where, in heaven's name, was the confident, capable Dr. Abigail Maitland now? Vainly, she tried to regain the cool control on which she prided herself.

"It's too much, isn't it?" she said, nervously smoothing the silky fabric of her dress.

Only in the sense that Christmas had come early this year, Kyle thought. Since she wasn't stepping back to allow him in, he took advantage of the moment to admire her. His eyes swept over her slowly.

"That all depends on your definition of 'too much.' I'd say you look terrific." He paused. "Are you going to invite me in?"

Feeling a little foolish, Abby opened the door wider. "Sure. Come in while I get my purse."

Kyle walked in, then glanced in her direction. He saw the uncertainty in her eyes. Because she seemed oddly unaware of the effect she was having on him—would have on any man with a pulse—he added, "I believe the expression is, 'You clean up nicely.'"

That coaxed a smile from her as she reached for the clutch purse she'd left on the overstuffed love seat in the living room. It was also where she'd left her shoes. Abby slipped them on as she looked at Kyle over her shoulder.

"Why, was I messy the other night?"

"No, not messy." He searched for the right word. "Professional."

Was that good or bad? She couldn't tell. "And now I'm an amateur?" Slipping on a light coat, she continued watching his face.

The amusement filtered from his eyes. "I'm sure the word *amateur* was never associated with you—not even the first time you were kissed."

Abby paused at the front door. "'Were kissed,'" she repeated. Considering the liberated times, she was surprised he'd phrase it that way. She prided herself on projecting the image of a woman who knew how to take charge. Never mind that she was a late-bloomer in this sort of situation. "What makes you think I wasn't the one who did the kissing?"

Very gently, he ushered her out the door. The plane would be waiting for them at the airport by now; he'd made sure the pilot had the time right. "Oh, I'm sure you were, but not initially."

Kyle opened the passenger door of the car for her, then waited until she was seated. "I think, even in this

day and age, there are some things about you, Abby
Maitland, that cling to tradition.'' He smiled when he
saw the protest in her eyes. It was for form's sake, he
was sure of it. ''You still let the man make some of the
first moves.'' She'd just proven it, he thought, by letting
him open the door for her rather than doing it herself.
''Not because you have to, but because you want to.
It's all about choice—and choosing what suits you.''

Abby waited until he rounded the hood and sat down
behind the wheel. ''I thought you were into telecommunications, not analysis.''

The car purred to life. ''Analysis is always the first
step, no matter what you're into.''

''That would kill spontaneity, wouldn't it?''

Kyle eased the car out onto the street. The area Abby
lived in was so peaceful, it was hard to believe that just
several hundred yards away lay the city of Austin.

''Analysis doesn't have to be conscious. It can take
place in the blink of an eye.'' He drove up to a light.
''You come up to the corner and analyze the situation
before hurrying across the street. Is the light red? Is it
green? Will I make it across, will I get run over? All
in the blink of an eye,'' he repeated. ''But it's still analysis.''

Abby always felt better when she knew what she was
up against. She'd done a little looking into Kyle
McDermott last night. It never ceased to surprise her
how much information she could glean from the Internet. ''They say that you can talk a polar bear into getting a fur coat. I'm beginning to believe it.''

He laughed shortly as he came to a major intersection. Here the traffic was lined up on all sides. He was
familiar with the article she was referring to, though the
description was highly exaggerated and at odds with the

way he felt about himself. "If that were true, I would have talked you into siding with me the other night."

"Maybe I was lucky, and it was an off night."

All things considered, he thought he might have given up too easily on that score. He was more convinced than ever that Abby Maitland could wield a great deal of influence over Marcie. "Meaning I should try again?"

You put your foot into it that time, Abby-girl. Way to go. "Maybe later."

She had to admit that the idea of mentally sparring with him did carry appeal. At least it would keep her mind from straying to places it had no business going.

Abby glanced out the window. Intimately familiar with the city she'd grown up in, she wasn't aware of any extraordinary seafood restaurant in the direction they were headed. Turning in her seat, she looked at Kyle and tried not to notice how rugged his profile was from this angle.

Again, that persistent flutter in her stomach.

"Just where is this restaurant?"

He looked amused at her question. "Hungry?"

"Curious." He was being awfully cagey, she thought. Why? "Is the restaurant far from here?"

"Distance," he informed her, an enigmatic smile playing on his lips, "is all relative."

Abby settled back in her seat, though she was far from relaxed. He *was* being cagey. Suspicions began to rise within her. Just where was he taking her, and would there be photographers waiting there when they arrived?

The butterflies went away.

CHAPTER EIGHT

IT SEEMED TO ABBY that they were driving into a more sparsely populated area away from the city. Straightening, she slid to the edge of her seat. Kyle was heading toward what looked to be a huge airplane hangar.

She turned to him. "What's that up ahead?"

Kyle had called the pilot earlier to make sure he would be available for the short trip. The Learjet was the only outward sign of true affluence he allowed himself and for the most part, he used it for business purposes. Just this once, however, the jet was going to be used for personal pleasure.

"An airfield."

She straightened in her seat. "And exactly why are we heading toward it?" Ahead of them, she watched the headlights cut through the surrounding darkness. A city-dweller at heart, sometimes it surprised Abby to see just how dark the night really was. "I thought you said we were going to a restaurant."

"We are."

Kyle brought the car to a stop, got out and came to her side.

Abby was already getting out. "Just where is this restaurant?"

He took her elbow, ushering her toward the plane. "On the outskirts of New Orleans." He nodded at the pilot. Someday, he promised himself, he was going to take flying lessons. "Evening, Beau, thanks for coming down."

Beau, tall, lean and dressed more for a night at the local movies than flying a CEO's plane, held the rear door of the jet open for them. There was an easy smile on the man's lips. "You're the one who signs the checks, Mr. McDermott."

Abby was still trying to assimilate the tidbit of information Kyle had thrown her way. She stared at him as she was led into the plane. "New Orleans? As in Louisiana?"

Right behind her, Kyle closed the door. The interior of the plane was more cozy than crammed. It hardly registered with Abby. What did was the smile on Kyle's lips. It was obvious that he knew he'd caught her off guard, and it pleased him. "You know of any other New Orleans?"

Her first thought was of her patients. "If someone pages me—"

He'd already considered that roadblock. "We can get back to Austin quickly enough." He tapped the side of the wall with affection, as if the plane was a favorite pet rather than a mode of commuting. "Flying's faster than driving."

Kyle gestured toward a seat and she took it, turning so that she could still look at him. New Orleans was awfully far to go for a meal. "Are you trying to impress me?"

"What I'm trying to do is get you to the restaurant." Joining her, he sat down, then relented. "Maybe a little," Kyle admitted as he buckled up. "How'm I doing?"

She hadn't expected him to be so honest. At least she

didn't have to worry that he was doing this because he wanted a share of *her* money.

Following his example, she buckled up. "I'll let you know when I taste the food."

Kyle pressed a button, signaling Beau that they were ready. He grinned at Abby, feeling oddly lighthearted. "Deal."

Within a few minutes, the jet began to taxi down the runway. "So tell me," Kyle said, "how are you holding up?"

She raised her brow suspiciously. "In what regard?"

"I've had a chance to glance at a newspaper since I last saw you." He saw that his words weren't well received. "The media can be brutal."

She shrugged, wanting to give as little importance to the invasive press as possible. "We're adjusting. Mother's taken temporary custody of the baby while we try to unravel the mystery and find out who he really is."

Getting custody hadn't been easy, even with the Maitland name. Strings had to be pulled and favors called in, but Abby had finally managed to do this for her mother. It had made her feel good.

"Meaning that the baby isn't—"

"Meaning that we have no answers yet. But we will."

THEY TOOK A RENTED SEDAN from the airfield and drove to the outskirts of New Orleans. Twilight flirted with the moon in store windows lining both sides of the streets. Kyle parked in a public lot, then took her hand as he led the way to the sidewalk. His fingers wrapped around hers, making her feel oddly safe in this place of gloomy shadows, where solemn eyes stared out at her from darkened doorways.

The restaurant wasn't even visible to her at first. Making their way down a narrow street, they turned into an even narrower alley.

The only hint that the door she saw was an entrance to a restaurant, and not the exit from some other establishment facing the boulevard, was the weather-beaten, faded sign that hung next to it. Decades ago there must have been vivid colors splashed across it; now there were only muted shades of brown bleeding into one another. The single word, Simon's, was hardly legible.

"You weren't kidding when you said run-down," Abby murmured, wondering if she was naive to feel safe with Kyle.

Kyle placed his hand on the scarred doorknob and opened the door. It had been a while since he'd been here, but the familiar feeling of homecoming was quick to find him.

"I also wasn't kidding about the food."

The door creaked as he pushed it farther open, bringing to Abby thoughts of haunted mansions and things that went *bump* in the night. She tried not to shiver. She didn't want to look like an idiot.

The lighting within Simon's came mainly from lit candles stuck in dusty wine bottles. She wondered if it was done to save on electricity, or if it was part of the eccentricity surrounding the restaurant and its owner. Either way, it made maneuvering tricky.

It also made the spiders easier to miss.

The tables and chairs all appeared to be mismatched. The people within the small, crammed space didn't seem to notice or care. The restaurant was packed.

"Looks like business is good tonight," Abby commented half to herself.

She felt his hand tighten over hers as he lowered his head closer to her. "Business," he whispered against her ear, "is always good."

Shock waves undulated through her as his breath skimmed along her cheek. It had to be the place, she told herself.

Before she could catch her breath, a tall, imposing black man with a barrel chest strode toward them. He wore a stained half apron that had been white too many years ago to remember, and a maroon shirt rolled up past his elbows, exposing massive biceps from years of heavy manual labor, and he looked to be close to six-and-a-half feet tall. As she raised her eyes to his scowling face, Abby thought that he was very possibly the most frightening man she had ever laid eyes on.

She squelched the impulse to step back as he reached them. Fierce, almost black eyes took slow, unabashed measure of her, as if to decide how he felt about her presence within his establishment.

Only then did the dark gaze silently shift to Kyle.

Kyle checked the urge to embrace the man, who was far older than he looked. He knew how Simon Le-Deveaux felt about public displays of affection. "Hello, Simon, I brought you a new soul to convert."

The wide mouth pressed itself into a single line as Simon regarded Abby again. "Don't need new souls. Got plenty of people coming to keep me busy all the day and night." The scowl deepened. "Where you bin? Thought you was dead, boy."

"Busy." And regretfully unable to spare the time to come here. The price of getting what you wanted, Kyle had thought more than once, was losing touch with what kept you going to get there. "Don't you read the business section?" He knew Simon felt a secret pride when things went well for people he had taken under his wing. The man had fed Kyle many times when his pockets had been as empty as his belly.

"Don't read. Don't have to." He was looking at Abby as he spoke. "What I need to know of life comes through my doors." He shrugged one wide shoulder, underlining his thought. "Or else it don't matter. You want your table?"

"Yes." Kyle looked over toward the window where he used to sit, studying and eating. It was occupied.

"Too bad." Simon gestured grandly in that general direction. At any given moment, he knew how many people were in his place and what they were having. "People sitting there. People who come regular-like, not like some." A hint of approval came into his eyes as they swept over Abby again. "She's pretty. Why's she with you?"

There was nothing like a visit to Simon's to make him feel like a kid again. Kyle found himself smiling as he slipped an arm around Abby's back. "It's a pity date."

Simon nodded, then turned, leading them off to the side to a table he kept free for special occasions. "She must have plenty, put up with you." He stopped, gesturing for them to be seated. "How's your sister—still going to school?"

The mention of Marcie made his smile tighten just a touch. He knew that Simon would pick up on it and not say anything. "She's taking a break."

Simon digested the information, nodding. "Make her put it to good use." He paused, as if debating whether to say anything further. Except that Simon never debated. "Not everybody need schooling. I got six grades, all I need. People still come whether I educated in brick buildings or not. You sit," he instructed Abby, pulling back the chair for her. His eyes danced as he regarded her. "I bring you something make you think you're in heaven, only better." The promise was made with relish.

Awed, Abby watched the man disappear into the kitchen. Noise and steam greeted his entrance when he pushed open the swinging door.

She let out a long breath. "He leaves quite an impression." Abby glanced down at the table, then around the room. "No menus?"

Kyle shook his head. "Simon says he knows what to serve a person just by looking at them."

That put the man one up on her. She didn't even know what she was in the mood for. But she had to admit that the aromas drifting through the restaurant were beginning to arouse her taste buds.

And the man sitting opposite her aroused other appetites. The candlelight, playing across his face, made him look sexier than she thought possible. Abby shifted her attention to the glass of water before her. "That could get insulting if he decides to set a crab dish in front of someone."

Kyle laughed. "Nobody picks a fight with Simon."

"I can understand why." The man cast an even more forbidding shadow when he spoke than when he merely looked at you in silence. She tried to imagine what he looked like smiling, and failed. "How did you ever find this place?" To say it was off the beaten path was an understatement.

Fragments of memories crowded his mind. Kyle reviewed them with affection. "It kind of found me. I went on a bender—my first and last," he added, in case she thought he made it a regular habit. The last thing he wanted was to appear as if he were his father's son. What he didn't add was that the incident had happened during a period when he had hit absolute rock bottom. "It was pouring rain, and I vaguely remember stumbling into a doorway. When I woke up, I was inside Simon's with Simon's scowling face and accusing eyes glaring down at me. Simon doesn't approve of drinking, thinks alcohol is the devil's way of getting even with man for picking God over Satan," he confided. "He gave me something for my hangover, something to eat, and a long lecture." His smile grew wider. "I used to come back whenever I could."

She'd been under the impression that he'd lived in Austin all his life. "Wasn't this a little out of the way for you?"

It was worth every step, every inconvenience he had had to put up with. Simon, like his restaurant, was one of a kind. "I went to college not too far from here." He remembered how sad he'd felt, leaving. It had taken the shine off graduating. "When I had to go back home to take care of things, I made coming here my one guilty pleasure. When you taste the food, you'll understand why."

She had a feeling that the food was only secondary when it came to Kyle's pilgrimages here. The thought of the bond between the successful businessman and the eccentric restaurateur created a warm feeling within Abby.

Simon was suddenly back, a large, steaming bowl of clams in his massive hands. He placed the bowl between them, but he directed his eyes toward Abby. "These are for you."

The bowl looked almost bottomless. She gazed up at him. "All of them?"

"You can let him have some if you want to share." He winked at her, a flash of white teeth contrasting against his midnight-dark skin. The deep voice lowered to an amused rumble. "I think maybe you won't."

Kyle was amazed. Usually it took a while before Simon would even deign to speak to someone new—certainly before he showed any sort of approval. That made Abby Maitland a very special lady. But then, he had come to suspect that himself.

"I think you just found yourself in a very exclusive club," Kyle told her. "I've been coming here for almost ten years and I've never seen Simon smile." The closest he'd witnessed was a lack of disapproval.

Simon took umbrage at what seemed like criticism. "That's because there's only your ugly face to look at. Now, you bring something better for me to see." And then the interlude was over. "Eat," he ordered her. "You will enjoy."

He wasn't moving, Abby noted. "Are you going to watch me?"

He crossed his arms before his chest, his eyes sealed to hers. "Yes."

Without realizing it, Abby ran the tip of her tongue over her lower lip. "Okay."

Battling self-consciousness, she gingerly took a clam and set it on her plate. Very carefully, she opened it. The two sides slid apart without effort, telling her that the clam had been previously opened. The moment her tongue came in contact with the tiny morsel, she realized this wasn't merely a plate of steamed clams. Each piece had been marinated in something that she couldn't put her finger on. Something incredibly delicious.

Swallowing, she looked at Simon with wonder. "Exquisite."

"Of course." He took the compliment as his due, but it was obvious that he was well pleased. He spared a last look in Kyle's direction. "She has taste." With that, he retreated to see to other patrons.

"I take it he's part of the entertainment?" she guessed, reaching for several more clams. They bumped against one another, seeking space on her plate.

Watching her, Kyle could only smile. A sense of vindication came over him. He knew he'd been right to bring her here. He'd wanted her to like Simon. And to have Simon like her. "He's more like part of the total experience," he said, taking a serving of clams for himself.

ABBY PUSHED THE PLATE away from her. This was clearly a case, she decided, of her eyes being much bigger than her stomach. But what a lovely way to go.

She could sense Kyle watching her, and felt the color rise to her cheeks.

"I'm not sure the plane's going to be able to take off again," she warned him. "I think I ate enough tonight to feed a small mid-western town." The pleasure didn't recede, even when faced with the whisper of a stomach that had been stretched farther than it ever had before. "I don't know what came over me—I just couldn't stop."

The words echoed in his head, teasing him. He could imagine her saying that about things other than food. Things done in the intimacy of a room with low music, dim lighting and soft sheets.

"Simon's food has that effect." Between the two of them, Kyle and Abby had finished the large bowl of clams. And the entrées that came after. Simon's did not serve desserts, but then, Simon's food left no room for dessert, so it was never missed. Kyle liked the contented, slightly sleepy look Abby wore. She'd look that way after making love, he thought, and wondered if he would ever make that discovery firsthand. "So, was I right?"

Abby took a deep breath. She doubted that she would ever feel hungry again. Right now, it didn't seem possible. "You were right."

He felt his smile rising to his eyes, spreading out from there. "I like a woman who isn't afraid to let a man be right once in a while."

Abby pretended to look lofty. "Men have been known to be right every so often. Even a stopped clock is right twice a day."

The candlelight was lovingly skimming along her skin, bathing her in golden hues. Making it incredibly difficult for Kyle not to lean over and kiss her. If he concentrated, he could almost taste her lips against his.

But all he'd allow himself to do was tangle his fingers in her hair and gently push back the single strand that had fallen forward. "Abby…"

His voice drifted over her, making her stomach tighten and her pulse accelerate in anticipation. It occurred to her, with a suddenness that startled her, that it had been a long time since she'd been kissed.

A long time since she'd wanted to be kissed.

His mouth was hardly two inches away from hers when the buzzing noise intruded, driving a sharp wedge between them.

The moment was gone, and Kyle drew back. The buzzing continued. He looked at the source of the offending noise. "I think your purse wants you."

Her heart was still hammering wildly in her throat. She wished she'd left her purse on his plane. Sometimes, being responsible had its drawbacks. Biting back a sigh, she straightened. She took out her pager and looked at the screen. It was her service—reality checking in on her. She fervently hoped one of her patients hadn't gone into early labor.

"I'll only be a minute. Does Simon have a telephone on the premises, or is that asking too much?" Given the man's nature, she wasn't sure he would approve of something as intrusive as a telephone.

"By the rest room." Shifting in his seat, Kyle pointed to the far side of the kitchen entrance. "It only works half the time," he warned her. "Simon's not much on technology."

The irony struck her. Kyle was on the cutting edge of technology, while Simon represented a world where menus seemed too complicated. "Must give the two of you lots to talk about," she murmured, rising. "I'll be just a minute."

He watched her hips move with merely a hint of sway as she walked away from him. She made his mouth water more than Simon's steamed clams.

Under his breath, he promised, "I'll be waiting—"

"What you do to scare her away?"

It didn't surprise Kyle to have Simon suddenly materialize behind him. For a big man, Simon moved almost soundlessly when he wanted to. It gave a share of credibility to the myth that Simon LeDeveaux's grandmother had been a witch.

"Nothing." Kyle drew his eyes away from Abby's disappearing form and turned to look at Simon. "She got a call on her pager. She's a doctor," he said, answering the unspoken question in Simon's eyes.

Simon nodded. "Nice class of people you run with these days. Not like the old days."

There were a few unsavory types in his past. People Kyle chose not to remember, now that his life had changed so drastically. He shrugged at the comment. "You're confusing me with someone else."

"Simon is never confused." His penetrating gaze narrowed on Kyle. "Smart-mouthed boy, think he got the world by the tail." A powerful hand shot out, grasping nothing, then slowly opened up again. "All he got in his hand is air." Simon looked at him knowingly. "Not like now." Finished, he nodded behind Kyle. "The lady, she coming back." He lowered his voice and the single word took on all the more emphasis. "Behave."

Overhearing, Abby looked at Kyle curiously as she took her seat again. "Did he just tell you to behave?"

"He figured I scared you away." Now that he thought of it, Simon had probably seen him leaning in to kiss her. He wondered if that was what Simon's warning was all about: If Kyle moved too quickly, he might frighten her away. But someone like Abby Maitland must be accustomed to men making moves on her. She was far too unsettlingly beautiful to have gone unnoticed. "So, is there an emergency?"

Abby thought of the phone call, and of the question tendered hesitantly, desperately. She couldn't help the grin that rose to her lips.

"No emergency. Turned out one of my patients over-dramatized the situation to get past my service. She just wanted to know if it was all right to make love with her husband even though she's six months pregnant." Her eyes skimmed over the table, lingering on the flickering candle. "Seems they just had a very romantic evening, but she wanted to check with me before things took their natural course." Abby laughed.

"What's so funny?"

"As soon as I said it was all right, she was gone in a flash. Almost didn't hang up the phone." Abby wasn't aware of the sigh that escaped her lips. "Wonder what they had for dinner."

"A healthy dose of oysters," he guessed. "Along with a large portion of love."

Evening flights, romantic dinners in restaurants completely off the beaten path. And the sentiments of a poet. Kyle seemed a far cry from the man who had sat so impatiently in her reception area the other day.

"Why, Kyle, you're a romantic. I would have pegged you as far too pragmatic."

Simon should have put them at a smaller table, he thought, leaning closer to her. "Goes to show that you can't always tell what's under the cover." He elaborated a little. "If you were to walk by the outside of this building without knowing the kind of food that was served here, your natural tendency would be to keep right on walking. And then you would have missed a great experience. Am I right?"

She tilted her head a little, studying him. "Yes. And right twice in one evening. I'm impressed."

The idea of taking her home with him, of making love to her slowly, savoring every kiss, every movement, appealed to him immensely. With luck, Marcie was asleep by now. Or, to be safe, there was always Abby's place. "Would you like me to go for three?"

This was where she should say, *Thank you, but I really should be getting home.* Or words to that effect. She had gone as far out on the limb as she should with a patient's brother. Yet instead, she heard herself saying, "I'm listening."

Her eyes mesmerized him. The way they widened when she looked up at him. Made a man feel taller than he was. "Why don't we get out of here?"

Without waiting for her answer, he wrapped his fingers around her hand and rose to his feet, drawing her with him. Kyle left a crisp hundred-dollar bill on the table, the way he always did when he ate here. It was far more than the meal had come to, but it was his way of thanking Simon for bringing a boy in out of the rain—in more ways than one.

From behind an old-fashioned cash register that had seen its zenith in the early sixties, Simon raised one benevolent hand high and waved them on their way.

Abby looked at the man over her shoulder as Kyle ushered her out. "Shouldn't we at least stop to say goodbye?"

But Kyle continued walking. "Simon doesn't like people saying goodbye. He says it means they won't be coming back." The door closed with finality behind them. "Where would you like to go now?"

Her eyes danced. "If I said Paris, would you take me there?"

"That all depends." He looked down at the little purse that swung from her shoulder. "Would your pager still work there?"

She laughed, then considered the question. "I don't know," she said honestly. Time for Cinderella to give back the coach and footmen. "I guess you'd better make it home, then."

There was a note of finality in her voice that told him the scenario he was playing out in his head wasn't to be, at least not tonight. He knew enough not to push. But he didn't want the evening to end, either.

They headed toward the car. "Why don't I make it Austin, but not home yet?"

"You're the one with the plane."

He stopped walking just short of the corner and looked at her. She didn't strike him as a woman who was willing to meekly hand the reins of a date over to her escort. Not willing to be put on, he didn't take the bait. "You do have a vote in this, you know."

Yes, she knew that. But just for now, she wanted to bury logic, which dictated that she go home and let the evening come to an end. "For the time being, I abstain."

In the end, though, because they both had full schedules the next day and the hour was late, they reluctantly decided to call it a night.

After deplaning at the airfield, Kyle took Abby home in his car. The trip back was filled with small talk and the music from the CD player in his car. Silences were wedged in between compact sentences, but they were neither pregnant nor uncomfortable. Instead, they fed a feeling of contentment that Kyle knew he would have been hard-pressed to understand if he'd stopped to examine it.

What he was, he discovered, was happy. Simply happy. The feeling had become so unfamiliar to him over the past couple of years that he almost didn't recognize it.

All he was aware of was Abby.

When he reached her house, they walked silently up to the doorway. He was holding her hand, he realized.

"I had a wonderful time," she said, "and if anything, you undersold the restaurant."

He wasn't interested in talking about the restaurant, or even Simon. "I'd like to see you again, Abby."

There was the space of a moment before she replied. "Marcie's next appointment is on Monday."

Their hands were still linked, and he slid his fingers between hers. "That's not what I meant."

She took a slow breath before answering. "I know what you meant."

"And?"

He saw hesitation in her eyes. Saw it and made up his mind not to let it ruin what had been an extremely pleasurable evening. Rather than hear her tell him all the reasons why she felt they would be better off not seeing each other again, he crooked his finger beneath her chin, raised it and lowered his lips to hers.

And touched off a discovery he was totally unprepared to make.

CHAPTER NINE

THIS YEAR'S FOURTH OF JULY celebration had been history for over two months now, yet someone had obviously forgotten to clear away a huge cache of unused fireworks. Because fireworks were what he found himself in the middle of right now. Brilliant fireworks, exploding in the night sky and setting it aglow with a rainbow of shining colors that lingered before drifting back to earth.

Fireworks. In his head as his arms tightened around Abby and the kiss deepened.

Fireworks. Deep in his soul.

And with them, heat. The kind of heat that came from standing too close to the fireplace. But he had no protective screen to hide behind. All he had was an overpowering reaction to the kiss that he'd begun. A reaction and a gnawing hunger.

And no breath to speak of.

Disoriented, he sank deeper into the unknown, reveling in it.

Abby had been on a vacation when she was barely out of her teens, where she and her friends had gone to Hawaii to enjoy the beaches. Reckless, wanting to live life to the fullest before she turned her mind to medical school, Abby had taken a dare and dived off a cliff.

For one long moment as she headed toward the sparkling water, her heart had felt as if it had been frozen in time, even as it pounded madly. The words *What have I done?* had echoed wildly in her brain.

Those words came to her now. Along with the same exhilaration, the same sheer terror and excitement.

At first his lips were gentler than the water she had swum in. But that gentleness faded as urgency grew. From him, from her, she wasn't sure. She didn't care. All she wanted to do was savor this wild, pulse-destroying moment before it slipped back into the realm of fantasy.

This had to be a fantasy. Nothing real felt this good.

She sighed against his mouth as he drew back slightly.

"Is that a yes?"

His voice was low, hoarse, as it reached her ear. His breath tickled and teased, and parts of her body tightened in anticipation.

She felt too numb to move. Bereft at the loss of his lips on hers.

Yet even now, Abby's conscience and sense of propriety were returning. They were always the first to take up their posts. She swallowed, hoping her voice wouldn't crack. "No, that's a 'We'll see.'"

He cupped her cheek, and his lips twisted in a grin. "Then I can't wait to find out what 'yes' feels like."

Yes was a word that every part of her body was silently screaming. It took a lot for her to ignore the entreaty. But she had to. She couldn't go out with him again. This was absolutely crazy, this feeling running rampant through her.

Abby took a step back, as if that would somehow help. "I really, really have to go." *Before I beg you to stay.* Her fingers searched frantically along the bottom of her purse, trying to locate her keys. Where had they gotten to? It wasn't that big a purse.

Relief flooded through her as her hand closed over the key ring. Quickly, praying her hand wouldn't shake and give her away, she thrust the key into the keyhole.

"Yeah, me, too." He made no move to give credence to his words, but simply stood there as if his shoes were glued in place.

Abby knew he wanted to go in with her. But she was sure he wouldn't press, even though there was a look in his eyes that told her he was just as affected by what had happened as she was.

Kyle's voice sounded behind her as she pulled open the front door. "I'll call you."

Abby barely nodded in acknowledgment. "Sure." The next second, she disappeared behind her door.

She closed it firmly, afraid that if she left it open another moment, she'd grab Kyle by his arm and drag him inside. The way she wanted to.

Her whole body was humming like a tuning fork. With her back against the door, Abby slid slowly down until she was sitting on the floor, a boneless puddle.

What had he done to her?

"You really, *really* should get out more, Abby-girl," she murmured under her breath.

But she couldn't stop tingling.

"SO, HOW WAS IT? Tell me everything, and I mean *everything*." Breathless from her brisk walk across the length of Maitland Maternity to reach the cafeteria, Dana sank down into the chair opposite Abby at the small table.

Though Abby had been deep in thought, Dana's sudden descent didn't startle her. She knew one of her friends would seek her out sooner than later, eager for details. Abby shrugged, playing with the cellophane wrapper of the unopened sandwich in front of her.

"There isn't anything to tell."

"Liar. I can see it in your eyes." Dana opened the wrapper on Abby's sandwich and broke off a corner. "They're glowing."

Abby nodded toward the ceiling. "They just changed the fluorescent bulbs in here."

Besides, she thought, picking at her sandwich, her eyes weren't "glowing," they were reflecting her bewilderment. Half a day later, she still hadn't been able to sort out just what had happened on her front step last night. Every time she thought about it, she only became more confused. How could she be reacting this strongly to a man she hardly knew? It wasn't like her.

Dana finished the corner in two small bites. "C'mon, Abby, have a heart. I need to live vicariously." Wiping her fingers with a napkin, she sighed. "Your brother's never going to see me as anything but his faithful girl Friday." She tossed the napkin aside and leaned in closer, a conspirator waiting to be filled in. "Talk to me. What's Kyle McDermott really like? I heard he was supposed to be all business."

Abby laughed shortly. "Well, he certainly meant business last night." The words had come out before she could think to suppress them. Dana's eyes grew huge with awe.

"Oh, wow, wait." She held her hand up, looking over toward the long self-serve counter. "Should I be ordering something cold to drink?"

Abby shook her head. "Only if you're thirsty." She wanted to bring the subject to a quick halt. "Look, it was just a nice evening, that's all. He took me out to a restaurant—''

"Details," Dana insisted. "When will you learn to share properly?" She shook her head, breaking off more of the sandwich. "I need details. Which one, where?"

If she closed her eyes, Abby could still see it. Still smell the aroma of the shimmering shrimp in lobster sauce that Simon had brought after the clams had been finished. "It was called Simon's."

Dana looked puzzled. "Doesn't sound familiar. Where did you say it was?"

Abby purposely avoided Dana's eyes. "In New Orleans," she murmured.

"New Orleans. He flew you to New Orleans. For dinner."

Abby could hear the awe in Dana's voice. "And you call that a 'nice' evening? My God, Abby, you are one hard date to impress. No wonder you don't go out much." The moment the words were out of her mouth, Dana gasped. "I'm so sorry. I didn't mean that the way it sounded." Reaching across the table, she placed her hand on Abby's wrist and squeezed. "I know why you don't go out."

"Because I'm busy."

The look in Abby's eyes dared Dana to contradict her. But they had been friends far too long to stand on ceremony or be intimidated by dark looks. "Because you're scared."

"I'm not scared." Abby raised her chin. She had neither the time nor the desire to be analyzed. "I dove off that cliff in Hawaii, remember? And you're the one who didn't want to go sky diving."

"I'm not talking about physical risks, and you know it," Dana argued. "You volunteer your free time in seedy neighborhoods that would make your brothers drag you out by the hair if they knew. There's no denying that you're one hell of a brave woman—physically." A small, sad smile flickered over her lips. "It's emotionally that you've become Chicken Little."

Dana meant well. Abby knew that. "Careful, before I get angry and peck at your shins."

"I'll chance it." Dana took her friend's hand in hers. "Abby, you're a wonderful person. Just because you had some rotten luck with that two-bit jerk doesn't mean you have to cut yourself off from the male population as a whole. He was one rotten apple. There are a lot more apples out there. And Kyle McDermott looks like a prize-winning one."

The metaphor made Abby think of the apple Snow White had been offered. One bite and the fairy-tale princess had been drugged. Just as Abby had been last night. But she was thinking clearly today. Thinking clearly and remembering just what had happened the last time she allowed herself to be dazzled.

Very gently, she drew her hand away from Dana's. "Ever since I can remember, I've had to be careful who I let into my life. At first I didn't want to believe that people wanted to be with me not because of what I was inside, but because of who I was, and who my father and mother were. But I learned differently. The hard way."

Pushing the remainder of her sandwich toward Dana, she took a sip of her diet cola. It didn't help cut the dryness in her throat.

"Having as much money as my family does is not just a blessing and a responsibility, it's a curse." The Maitlands had been able to accomplish a great deal of good with the money they'd been given, but it had also imprisoned them in a glass cage. At times, Abby tended to forget that. But not now. "You're never really sure what people want from you."

Dana wasn't naive enough to argue the point. She simply said, "You've got more than a few people who care about you, Abby."

Shaking herself from the mood that was overtaking her, Abby smiled. "Yes, I do, and I'm very fortunate in that. I don't have to be some poor little rich girl, feeling left out of life. My work, my family and the friends I have keep my life more than full."

If Dana heard the finality in Abby's voice, she ignored it. "How about those nights when you're awake?" she pressed. "And alone in bed?"

Abby laughed. "If I minded being alone in bed, I'd get another pet. Like Chester."

Dana frowned. "Chester was a dog."

"A dog who thought he was part of the family."

The large Labrador had been given to Abby by her brothers for protection. Any burglar breaking in was guaranteed to immediately get slobbered to death. She'd had the dog for seven years before he died. Maybe that was it: she just missed the dog's companionship.

"You talked me into it."

"What? Giving Kyle a fair chance?" Dana asked hopefully.

"No, getting another dog."

Dana made a strangling noise.

Just then, the pager at Abby's waist went off. Secretly relieved, she glanced down to get the number. "Saved by the beep."

"I'm not giving up on you, you know," Dana vowed as Abby rose from the table. "One of us needs a warm male in our lives."

That being the case, Abby would gladly volunteer her friend. It was simpler that way. "I'll see what I can do about waking up that lunkhead brother of mine."

For a second, Dana looked wistful. "If wishes were horses…"

Abby recalled the old saying. *…then beggars would ride.* "Some beggars rode." She winked, backing away from the table. "But they first had to tame the horse they found. Gotta run."

"As always."

Dana's voice followed her out of the cafeteria, and Abby knew her friend wasn't just referring to her busy schedule.

I'LL CALL YOU.

Annoyed with herself, Abby closed the folder in her hands. Why was that line haunting her? It was a throwaway that every man handed a woman, even when he wasn't interested.

Especially when he wasn't interested, she amended with feeling. It made parting that much less awkward. A lot better than saying *Only when hell freezes over.*

She'd had a nice time but it was now in her past. What was the problem?

The problem was that she was restless and she had no idea why. Why was this feeling of waiting for something gnawing away at her? It wasn't as if Kyle had broken a date with her. There was no date. They hadn't even made tentative plans.

She dropped the folder into the To Be Filed pile and blew at the wayward strand of hair that fell into her eyes. It fell back down. Muttering an oath, she pushed it behind her ear.

He'd said he wanted to see her, and she'd said maybe. That put the ball in his court, didn't it?

Abby stared out the window at the almost filled parking lot, seeing only the ghost of her reflection looking back.

"Face it, Abby-girl," she murmured. "It's been so long since you played, you don't even remember the rules of the game."

Turning from the window, she shoved her fisted hands deep into her pockets. It was probably better this way. *Was* better this way. She wouldn't have to hold him suspect for everything he did, examine every word he said for hidden meanings.

Granted, the man was head of a multimillion-dollar company and probably wouldn't be after her for her money—although there was no rule that said the rich didn't want to get richer. But there were more things than just money involved. His wealth was newly acquired. Could he turn a blind eye to the prestige that being associated with the Maitlands of Austin would bring?

And even if money and prestige meant nothing to him, there was yet another ulterior motive that might bother her if he continued to try to romance her. Would he be going out with her for her company, or in order to persuade her to exercise her influence over his sister?

Now that she thought of it, there was no denying that he'd retreated far too easily for a man who had the reputation of being a bulldog when he went after something. And Marcie's welfare was of tantamount importance to him.

Abby was making herself crazy. What did it matter, anyway? The man hadn't called.

It had been several days since they'd gone out. Three

days to be exact, and there hadn't been so much as a halfhearted attempt on his part to initiate phone tag.

To top it off, Marcie had canceled her appointment that morning, since her allergies had flared up. Abby had recommended a suitable medication and had had Lisa call Marcie with it. It was the closest contact she'd had to either McDermott since Kyle had left her on her doorstep.

With Marcie's cancellation, Abby's morning schedule had become lighter than usual. And with no unscheduled deliveries or emergencies to fill up the gap, Abby found herself with time on her hands.

Time to think.

Bad move.

She needed something to take her mind off herself and back onto important things. Like the foundling. Almost a week had gone by, and they were no closer to uncovering the identity of the woman who had left him there or the father who had sired him.

What they had learned was the identity of every reporter, photographer and camera jockey in the metropolitan area. The media horde had camped out on the clinic's front lawn the first couple of days, until her mother had gotten a court order forcing them back to at least the parking lot, saying they were obstructing the normal flow of a vital service area.

In the last couple of days, the number had thinned considerably, but Abby knew the family was by no means in the clear yet. These reporters could and would pop out of the woodwork when she least expected it.

Abby needed a break.

Calling out to Lisa to tell her where she could be found, Abby left by the rear office door. She took the elevator down to the day care center that Beth ran on the premises. It had been almost a day since she had seen the infant boy who had stirred up such a furor by his very existence. She wanted to look in on her potential nephew and see how he was getting along.

After the woman from Social Services had granted her mother temporary custody, Megan had had one of the rooms at the mansion converted into a lavish nursery. If he was a Maitland, Abby thought with a smile, he would be one in style.

Evenings, he spent at the house with her mother, but days, he spent at the Maitland day care.

Her mother had insisted on it. It was more than just a passing whim. Megan spent most of her time at the clinic, anyway, and there was no telling what danger the baby might be exposed to from the press or anyone else. Abby knew they'd all feel better having the clinic's security team to fall back on. *Kidnapping* was an ugly word, but one the Maitlands had learned to live with.

As always, a wave of noise, joyful for the most part, greeted her as she opened the door to the center. Beth had two women, all certified in preschool care, working for her. Between teachers and children, Abby would have put the count for the day care at upward of twenty-five. The spacious, cheerfully decorated room thrummed with activity.

Seeing Beth, Abby made her way toward her younger sister. "So, how's our big guy doing?"

Surprised, Beth turned around to face her, a fistful of stubby crayons in her hand. She flashed a grin. "Hi, Abby. If you mean the mystery baby, he's happy as a clam." She deposited the crayons into a large container on a nearby table. Two of the older children, around age four, began dividing the loot between them.

It was about time the baby had a name, Abby

thought. As far as she knew, no one in the family had ventured to suggest one. That might be seen by the press as an admission that the boy was indeed a Maitland.

But didn't keeping him here amount to the same thing? Abby looked down at the small face in the bassinet. Was that a smile, or just the aftereffects of breakfast? She preferred the first possibility.

"You know, we have to call him something. 'Baby' is beginning to wear thin." She glanced around at the other inhabitants of the room, some hardly more than babies themselves. "And it could be a bit confusing."

"Mother's taken to calling him Cody," Beth told her. "Said something about it suiting him. Don't ask me why."

"Cody," Abby repeated. "Cody." She rolled the name around on her tongue, then smiled. "She's right, it does."

"Hi, Cody." Unable to resist, Beth tickled the baby along his thigh. Chubby little legs pumped in response as he gurgled happily. "Ford said he can't be more than about five weeks old."

"Five weeks." Abby shook her head as she picked the baby up and cuddled him against her. "It would kill me to be separated from my baby when he was only five weeks old." Holding him to her, she breathed in the delightful scent of baby powder and shampoo, and felt something maternal stir within her. "Or any age," she amended softly, addressing the words to the baby.

Beth stood back, watching her. When Abby raised her eyes to her quizzically, Beth said, "You look good holding him in your arms. When are you going to have one of your own?"

"Someday." The word came out on a sigh. The nebulous *someday*. Then Abby shrugged. That was being wistful, and she had always been one to face reality. The reality was that she had no time for any more of a family than she already had.

"What kind of a mother would I make, what with the hours I keep and running around the way I do?"

There wasn't a moment's hesitation. "A darn good one." Beth placed her hand on Abby's shoulder. "You and I both know that the most important ingredient in any relationship, with little people or big ones," she added significantly, "is love, and you've got that to spare."

Abby was about to answer when the sound of raised voices in the hallway intruded into the brightly lit room.

Liz, Beth's assistant, was angrily shouting at someone. "I said you can't go in there."

The someone obviously wasn't about to listen. From the sound of his voice, Abby surmised that the man Liz was trying to keep out was a great deal larger than Liz, who weighed approximately ninety-eight pounds with both pockets filled with rocks.

"Sorry, lady, got a job to do. Haven't you ever heard of the First Amendment? Guarantees freedom of the press."

A sinking sensation penetrated as Abby looked at her sister. "It's like being infested with roaches. No matter how much you spray, they keep coming back.

The next moment, a stocky man in a brown-and-beige plaid shirt that looked one size too small for him came bursting into the room. He was brandishing a camera like a weapon. The camera whirled as he scanned everything in sight, afraid of overlooking the very thing he'd come to capture on film.

Beth backed up, not knowing who to shield first. The

children, scattered about the room at the various play stations, all looked up at the disturbance.

Holding the baby close to her, Abby turned away. But her only exit was blocked by the cameraman, and she knew there was little chance of protecting the baby from the video camera. No matter which way she turned, the man was there. For a heavyset man, he was surprisingly agile.

"How did you get in here?" she demanded.

And where was Security when you needed them? Out of the corner of her eye, Abby saw Liz racing to the back desk and the telephone.

"Ingenuity's part of the game, lady. C'mon, stop turning around. Everybody wants to see what this little guy looks like up close and personal." Though the cameraman was matching her move for move, he was still just managing to miss the shot he wanted. His patience began to grow thin. "The sooner I get what I came for, the sooner I'll be out of your hair."

Abby felt her temper threaten to snap despite the fact that the man outweighed her by what appeared to be a hundred pounds. It didn't change the fact that he was hounding a defenseless baby. "You people are never out of our hair. Get out before I have Security call the police."

The threat of police intervention seemed to leave the man completely unfazed.

"I can get those pictures before the boys in blue come to your rescue. This isn't for some cheesy rag," he insisted. "It's for *Tattle Today*. That's TV." He said the name as if it would actually make a difference to her. "You play nice with them, and they'll—"

"Get slapped with a lawsuit for harassment," she shot back, her eyes blazing. "Get out of here. Now.

You're frightening the children.'' It wasn't a request; it was a demand.

The man reached out one hand to forcibly turn her so he could take a clear shot, but instead, found himself being roughly spun around.

"You heard the lady. She said to get out. I'm not going to ask you as nicely as she did. Now *move it!*''

His head slightly rattled by the fast maneuver, the cameraman found himself looking straight into Kyle's eyes. They were cold, steely.

The man's fingers tightened around his camera. Recognition dawned and took hold. Instead of backing off, he saw a new possibility. And a bigger payoff. "Kyle McDermott. This *is* getting bigger all the time, just like Chelsea said it would. How about the two of you together? With the baby. Readers're going to love it.''

His eyes darted from Kyle's face to Abby's and back again.

Kyle fought the very real desire to rearrange the placement of the man's nose. It had been a long time since he'd fought off such a strong urge. His hand tightened on the man's shirt. "How about a shot of you leaving the room? Horizontally, if you prefer.''

The man's breathing was becoming audible. "You don't scare me.''

"Really?'' Kyle cocked his head as if studying the other man with growing interest. "Because right now, I scare myself. Now get out before I do something you'll regret.'' With that, Kyle released him, with a shove.

The man stumbled backward, catching himself just in time. "I've got a perfect right—''

The smile that peeled back Kyle's lips was slow, cold. He rubbed his knuckles with his left hand. "So do I, they tell me.'' His eyes never left the other man's face. ''Silver gloves, two years in a row. Middle-weight division.''

Cursing, the man scurried away.

CHAPTER TEN

"IS THAT TRUE?"

Kyle turned around to face Abby, once he was fairly certain that the man wasn't returning. "Is what true?"

Abby looked at him dubiously. "Silver gloves, two years in a row?"

He laughed. "I've never been in the ring in my life. But that guy sure bought it."

"You're pretty scary when you want to be," Abby said. She placed Cody back in his bassinet, and the tension began to break. Behind her, Beth and the others were letting out sighs of relief. The children went back to the games they were playing.

A smile touched Kyle's lips. She'd been pretty tough herself with that cameraman before he'd stepped in. "So are you," he observed.

His eyes swept over her. He was finding more and more things that attracted him to Abby Maitland. And therein lay the problem.

One of his problems, he amended silently.

But how he felt about Abby hadn't been what brought him here today. "You looked as if you were ready to go head to head with that character if I hadn't come along." There was bravery, and then there was stupidity. He wondered if she knew the difference. "Didn't anyone ever explain the laws of physics to you?"

She raised her eyes to his. "Specifically?"

Kyle moved a little closer to her, sparing only a glance at the baby in the bassinet. So that was what all the commotion was about.

"Specifically, that Neanderthal men, especially ones who outweigh you, cannot be taken on by little, albeit lovely, lady doctors."

His eyes smiled at her as he said it, but Abby knew he was serious. Perhaps she should have been more cautious, but there was no way she was about to show any signs of fear around that miserable excuse for a human being. There was a time and a place for the news media, but it did not involve harassing an innocent baby.

"I guess it's lucky for me that the cavalry came in just when it did."

Kyle wondered if she was aware that she raised her chin like a fighter as she tried to bluff her way out. For a second, he forgot what had brought him here, forgot the man he'd all but physically thrown out of the day care in front of a roomful of pint-size witnesses. Humor played on his lips.

"Lucky."

Abby's heart settled down and her curiosity became aroused. She'd never expected to see Kyle in here. "And just why did you happen to pick this minute to ride to the rescue?"

"You weren't being threatened before," he quipped, then held up his hand before she could say anything. "And because I need you."

He couldn't mean that the way it sounded, but a warm rush dashed up her spine, anyway. Out of the corner of her eye, Abby saw Beth's eyes open wide.

The security guard picked that moment to stick his head in, mercifully allowing her a second to find her tongue. A tall, slightly balding man with just a hint of a paunch beginning, he quickly scanned the room, his eyes resting on Kyle. "Heard there was some trouble here, Ms…Dr. Maitland."

Abby smiled at the way the security guard addressed both her and her sister. She turned to Beth to see whether she wanted to deal with explanations, but Beth shook her head.

"I'll leave it to you, Abby, if you don't mind. I've got to check on the kids' lunches."

Abby turned back to the guard. "It's all over with now, Mike," she told him. She nodded toward Kyle. "Thanks to Mr. McDermott." But Kyle wouldn't be here if there was a next time. "I know your men can't stop everyone, but if you see someone with a camera, and it's not that cute, throwaway kind meant to commemorate the moment, ask for some ID, all right?" She crossed to the guard, lowering her voice. Abby didn't want to take a chance on any tales being carried out of the center on little feet. "We just had one of Chelsea Markum's snoops here, trying to get tape of the baby." Her eyes strayed back toward the bassinet. Even if he wasn't a Maitland, he didn't deserve to have flashes going off in his face. "The day care center should be a secure place."

"Absolutely," the man promised solemnly. "Won't happen again."

She half expected him to click his heels. Mike Salinger took his job very seriously. "I know that it won't. Thanks, Mike."

With a brief nod, Mike left. It was easy for Kyle to see that the other man was smitten with Abby. Mentally, Kyle tipped his hat to the departing security guard. *Got good taste, fella.*

Kyle turned toward Abby. The woman had a very

light touch. People in her position were known not to. He admired a fair hand as much as he did courage. "Very nice. You got your point across without stepping on his feelings."

"No need for that." Abby hated people who threw their weight around just because they could. "I want help, not enemies." She moved over to the side, where they could talk without one of Beth's helpers overhearing. "You said something about needing me." Why did her pulse do that tiny little flip-flop when she raised her eyes to his? After all, she'd just taken on a brute without so much as a shaky breath. "I assume that it's on a professional basis."

It wouldn't be right, Kyle thought, to kiss her here in front of everyone. That wasn't why he'd come looking for her. But that was what he now wanted, he realized.

When he spoke, the words came from a suddenly dry throat. "Does it have to?"

Abby shrugged, trying to seem indifferent when she was anything but. What *was* it about this man that rippled her still waters so?

With effort, she struggled to sound flippant. Her eyes skimmed over his hands quickly before returning to his face. "Well, you haven't made good on your parting phrase, and your hands seem sufficiently agile enough to be able to press buttons on a telephone. If my number escaped you, I'm in the book. Or you could have asked Marcie."

The sound of his sister's name elicited a flood of feeling—and reminded him why he'd suddenly taken off in the middle of a day crowded with appointments. "Marcie's the reason I'm here."

Abby searched his face. "Is something wrong?"

"That depends on your point of view. Hers, no. Mine, yes." He noticed one of the women looking their way with barely suppressed curiosity on her face. Without thinking, he took Abby's arm. "Look, is there somewhere we can go?" He couldn't remember if he'd seen a coffee shop in the area. "Somewhere I can buy you a cup of indecently priced coffee with a fancy name so that you have something to do with your hands while I pour out my guts?"

It wasn't a pretty picture, but he got his point across quickly. "Sounds like we shouldn't stray too far from the hospital." Abby glanced at her watch. "In any case, I have another appointment in twenty minutes." She thought for half a second. "How about the cafeteria? The coffee's reasonably priced and it only comes with sugar or cream, but other than that, it should serve your purpose."

He nodded. "I'm a little short on time myself."

And in a crowded cafeteria, where her friends and colleagues were bound to be passing through, he wouldn't be tempted to put his hand over hers, to apologize for not calling or to tell her the real reason why. Things like that were best left unconfessed. Knowing wouldn't do either of them any good.

Releasing her arm, he gestured toward the door. "Lead the way."

Abby went out first, ignoring her sister's wide grin as she left the day care.

"So what's this about Marcie?" Abby asked as soon as they were seated at a tiny table nestled in a corner near a tall, potted palm. She studied his face. "She's not really suffering from allergies, is she?" His brow rose quizzically. He probably didn't know about the phone call his sister had made this morning. "That was the reason she gave for breaking her appointment today."

"No, no allergy attack. More like a Kyle attack," he muttered under his breath.

Abby raised the cup to her lips, waiting. "And that would be…?"

He didn't really like letting someone know his personal business. Other than Marcie, Simon had been the only person he'd ever allowed close to him. Even this partial baring of his soul was difficult for him.

"We had an argument last night." Kyle swallowed a deep gulp of the hot coffee, letting it settle before continuing. "The last in a long line. I swear, ever since she turned sixteen…"

Annoyed with himself for straying, he blew out a breath. There was no point in rehashing things that couldn't be changed.

Kyle could feel her eyes on his face, waiting until he chose his moment, his words. He plowed ahead. "Anyway, the upshot of our latest argument is that she's determined to move out." She'd threatened that before, but this time, he knew she meant it. There was something in her tone, something that said she'd reached the end of her rope. "I can't handcuff her to the banister." The growled statement was half lament.

Abby's lips curved behind her paper cup. "There are laws," she pointed out dryly.

Why couldn't the law tell him how to deal with one hotheaded pregnant woman? "Well, short of handcuffing her, I can't get her to change her mind and stay."

The look in his eyes said he was hoping Abby could work a miracle. But she needed more information than he'd given her. "What was it that you said to set off this explosion?"

Kyle looked away. "Nothing." The word was bitten off and tossed in her direction.

She took no offense at his mood. She knew she had nothing to do with it. "Had to be something," she pressed, waiting.

After draining the rest of his coffee, he crushed the cup in his hand. Abby wondered who he was angrier with—himself, or Marcie for putting him through this. "I did the typical father thing." Kyle left the sentence dangling.

Abby set her cup down, slightly amused. "I'm not up on my typical father things. You're going to have to lead me through this."

The faint scent of her perfume was distracting him. Kyle struggled to focus. "I said, 'As long as you're living under my roof…'"

The classic line, guaranteed to set any recipient off like a Roman candle. "Oh. So now she's not going to be living under your roof."

He laughed shortly. When was he going to learn to rein in his temper with Marcie? It never got him anywhere. "That's the general idea." He turned his appeal up several degrees. "She has nowhere to go, Abby. And even if she did, I don't want her going there."

That, too, was typical, she thought. Her voice was kind, soft. And logical. "Did you ever consider that it's not your decision to make?"

He shook his head adamantly. "She's just a kid—"

Abby held up a finger, stopping him. "She's eighteen. That's old enough to be considered an adult. And in many ways, she is." And then she smiled. She used to butt heads with R.J. and even Mitchell on occasion when she was growing up. She both resented and secretly liked it when they took on the role of her big brother-protector. She suspected Marcie felt the same way. "Just not when it comes to talking with you. Note the word *with*," she pointed out.

"Yeah, I noted it," he said grudgingly. "I just can't seem to remember it when we're together." He looked at Abby for understanding and almost found himself getting lost in eyes that had no business being as blue as they were. "It's as if everything that's reasonable within me disappears as soon as I open my mouth."

Folding her hands on the table, Abby looked at him. She wondered if Marcie had a clue how fortunate she was to have someone care about her so much. There were girls who came through her doors—girls who had been thrown out by their families, or who had never even known their families—who would have killed to change places with Marcie McDermott.

"And what is it that you want from me?"

The question, coupled with the look in her eyes, brought Kyle up short, and he almost told her the thing that was hovering in his mind, that had been lingering there since he'd taken her out. Since he'd kissed her.

But this wasn't about him. It was about Marcie and what was best for her.

"I want you to come with me and talk to her, tell her not to go." His voice began to rise with feeling. "That she'd be stupid to go so close to giving birth—"

Abby laid her hand on his. The outpouring of words ceased. She smiled gently. "I think we can skip the word *stupid*."

Kyle shrugged helplessly. "Use any words you want—just get her to change her mind." And then his eyes met hers, and the bravado, the anger melted. His fears pushed forward. Marcie would leave just to show him she could. And he didn't want to be shown. "Please."

The word undid her. "Well, I have a patient in a few minutes, and like I said, I don't usually butt into my patients' personal lives." She paused. The look in his eyes got to her. "Except for a good cause. And I'm free after the patient leaves if you want me to go see Marcie."

He brought her hands to his lips before he thought better of it, before the reserve he'd schooled himself in caught up to him. "I owe you."

Desire came out of nowhere, surprising her. Throwing her off balance. Again.

"Make another donation." She looked down at the powerful hands that still held hers. "You'd better let go of my hands, unless you want to land on the cover of some tabloid." Abby pretended to glance around. "You never know where the paparazzi are hiding."

He released her hands, but not the guilt that was burrowing deep within him. He'd acted cowardly before, then tried to absolve himself because of all the things he had crowding his life, demanding his attention. There was no excuse.

"About not calling, Abby…"

She shook her head. She didn't want him feeling indebted to her. Debt wasn't a reason to make things right. "You don't owe me an explanation. I was out of line before for mentioning it."

He refused to let her shrug it off. Instead, he forced her to look at him. "No, I was out of line for not calling. It's just that, well, I wanted to see you."

She stared at him. That wasn't quite the excuse she'd

been anticipating. "So you didn't call. Somehow, I fail to connect the dots here."

She was putting herself out to help him. He owed her honesty if nothing else, even if it made him uncomfortable. "I wanted to call you too much. I don't like wanting something too much." He wasn't good with words, not when they really counted. "Not personally."

Abby slowly let out a breath. She understood. In a way. "So I guess it's up to me to make you want it a little less."

The smile that came to his lips was rueful. "Something like that." Allowing himself just a touch, he curved his fingers along her cheek. It reminded him of the other night. Of lips that left him wanting more. "You could try not looking quite so desirable."

Abby raised her brows. "And give up my lifelong dream to be a *femme fatale?* Never." Relaxed now, she flashed a smile as she rose from the table. Her tone was light and breezy, meant to make him feel secure. "We both had a nice time, and if we go out again, if we're lucky, we'll have a nice time again. But there's nothing more to it than that. Now, if you'll excuse me, I've got to run."

But there *was* something more to it than that, he thought as he watched her hurry away from him. A great deal more.

"WHY DO YOU keep dragging her into this?" Marcie demanded hotly, her hands on her hips as she faced her brother.

Behind her, on her bed, shoved in between the dolls Kyle had given her at various stages of her life, was a suitcase that was almost filled with her clothes. A suitcase she was about to shut, Kyle figured, when he had walked into her room, bringing reinforcements with him.

Marcie resented the intrusion. Resented his trying to turn her doctor against her. And resented Abby for being part of this.

She pressed her lips together, struggling to be civil. "Dr. Maitland, I'm sorry my brother dragooned you into this." Her brown eyes flashed as she looked at Kyle. "He just can't stand it that his almighty powers of persuasion hold no magic within these walls." Marcie waved her hand around the room, then looked at Abby. "I already made another appointment for Friday. I'll see you then. And as for you—" she glared at Kyle "—you're off the hook." She turned her back on them both, and began throwing the last of her clothes into the suitcase. "You don't have to be my coach anymore." With an angry slap, she shut the lid. "Happy?"

Part of Kyle regretted bringing Abby into this, to see and hear this display. But she was here, and he looked at her now, confident that she could at least understand what he was putting up with.

"You see? I can't reason with her." He pulled the suitcase out of Marcie's hands and threw it back on the bed. "She's impossible."

Deftly, Abby stepped in between the two, using her body as a barrier.

"I'm impossible? *I'm* impossible?" Marcie shouted, standing on her toes so that she could see him over Abby's shoulder.

"Yes, you're impossible," Kyle shot back. "And furthermore—"

Putting two fingers into her mouth the way Jake had taught her when they were kids, Abby whistled loud and long. Long enough to break in between the warring words and bring about a momentary, stunned silence.

Both McDermotts looked at her.

Finally. Standing beside Marcie, Abby turned to look at Kyle. "If we could call a temporary truce to the War of the Roses here, I'd like to have a few words with Marcie. That is why you asked me to come, isn't it?"

For a flicker of a second, he felt outnumbered. But that, he told himself, was only because of where Abby was standing. He'd brought her to help and he had every confidence that she would. She, at least, was a sensible female.

He gestured for her to begin. "Go ahead."

"Alone." Abby had no intention of talking to Marcie while Kyle hovered over them.

He hesitated, debating, then retreated because he had no choice. "Fine," he murmured. "I'll be—"

"Downstairs in the living room," Abby instructed him, knowing that he wanted to be closer. But she needed Marcie to feel that they had privacy. The girl wouldn't talk to her otherwise. "I know where to find you when I need you. I've a keen sense of direction."

Murmuring something unintelligible, Kyle left the room.

Only when he was gone, with the door closed behind him, did Abby turn to face Marcie. "All right, want to talk?"

The rebellious strain didn't abate immediately. "No."

Abby wasn't going to leave the room until everything was ironed out. She was prepared to wait the girl out. "All right, then I will." She gestured to the bed. "Sit, please."

Marcie opened her mouth to protest.

Abby's eyes narrowed only a fraction of an inch. "Sit."

There was something in the tone that was not to be trifled with. Marcie did as she was told. "Yes, Doctor."

The salutation was far too subservient to suit Abby. "Abby will do, I'm in my civilian clothes." Seeing a hint of a smile on the girl's lips, Abby officially began the peace talks. "Marcie, your brother loves you."

Marcie tossed her hair over her shoulder, stared out the window. She refused to look at Abby. "He certainly has a funny way of showing it."

Abby didn't have to see her face to know the tears were there. Marcie was not all that different from the way she'd been at the same age.

"Cut him a little slack," she coaxed. "He's a man. They stumble through this love thing all their lives, and if they get it right half the time, they're lucky."

Marcie looked at her, surprised at the turn in the conversation.

"It doesn't change the way they feel, though. Or the way Kyle feels," Abby added softly. "Your brother took time off from work to come to see me about you." That alone should speak volumes to the girl.

Her hand on her heart, she rolled her eyes to the ceiling. "So for once he puts me first. Should I faint or just give him my firstborn? No, wait, he *wants* my firstborn, so I guess my choices are easy, right? I stay here, give him my baby, and after twenty years, my hair'll be long enough to escape from the tower."

When Abby made no comment, Marcie looked at her.

"Got it out of your system yet?" Abby asked.

Marcie flushed. "Sorry."

"No need to be sorry. He makes you angry, I can

appreciate that. But it's only because he's trying so hard to make things right.''

"*His* right," Marcie pointed out with feeling.

Abby wasn't so removed from her own teens that she couldn't understand the frustration Marcie was going through. The young woman was too intense now to know that things would level out. "Nobody's arguing with that, honey. But sometimes his right *is* right.''

Marcie looked at her in surprise. "You think I should give up my baby?''

"No.''

The teenager frowned. "That I should marry Billy?''

"Not if you don't want to.''

"Then what?'' Marcie appeared momentarily stymied. "Stay here?'' she guessed.

Abby grinned. "Bingo.'' Abby appealed to her common sense. "Marcie, you're going to be having your baby soon. Never mind the pioneer legends of squatting in the field and then going on to pick the wheat. Giving birth is hard on a woman's body. Harder on some than on others, and we don't know just what your body can or can't take.''

Her eyes held Marcie's and she could see that she was getting through. Marcie really didn't want to leave; her threat was just the result of the growing rift between her and her brother.

"You're going to be having your hands full with getting back on your feet and being a new mom. Don't add looking for a place to stay and setting up housekeeping to the mix.'' For good measure, Abby threw in the clincher. "You decide you want to move out in three months, fine. I'll even help you look. But not now. And not like this. With hot words separating the two of you.''

Marcie stubbornly clung to her anger. "That's his fault."

But Abby knew all the ins and outs of that. "You can't have an argument by yourself." She grinned at Marcie, then grew serious. "You're no pushover, Marcie. You're not about to let anyone run over you or railroad you into doing what you don't want to. And I'm not saying that he probably didn't pull rank on you." As a matter of fact, she was willing to bet on it. "But Kyle does love you. You're all he talks about."

Abby could see that she'd struck deep.

"Don't get me wrong, Dr.—Abby, I love my brother. I love him a great deal and I have the utmost respect for him. He raised me, made sacrifices I don't know if I could have made in his place. I owe him everything. But most of all, I owe him a well-adjusted person who deserves those things he did for her. I can't be that way if I let myself be bullied into doing what I don't feel is right…"

Abby grinned. The girl really did have quite a head on her shoulders. Kyle could do with a little less shouting and a little more listening. "I bet you were good at riddles as a kid, weren't you?"

"Pretty good," Marcie admitted. A smile sneaked in.

Abby slipped her arm around the girl, more big sister than physician. "So, no moving out for now?"

Marcie glanced at the suitcase Kyle had left standing by the door. She raised her eyes to Abby. "I really didn't want to leave."

"I didn't think so." And then she saw the dismay come suddenly into Marcie's eyes. "What?"

"I told him he didn't have to be a coach anymore."

Abby breathed a sigh of relief. "Leave that to me."

She winked. "I'll make it part of the treaty negotiations."

Impulsively, Marcie hugged her. "Abby, you're the best."

Abby returned her hug, pleased at having resolved the problem—at least for the moment. "I try, Marcie. I surely do try."

CHAPTER ELEVEN

KYLE'S BACK WAS TO HER when she entered the living room. Even standing still, looking into the dormant fireplace, the man made her think of a caged animal.

That had been her first impression of him. A sexy, caged animal. Given that, it surprised her that he was capable of displaying any sort of patience at all.

For a second, because he wasn't looking in her direction, she indulged herself and took full measure of him. Tall, dark, handsome and rich. With qualifications like that, the man should have been working his way through his third marriage by now. It was rather amazing that he wasn't.

But then, Marcie had said Kyle was married to his career.

"She doesn't want to leave."

Kyle swung around at the sound of her voice. Forced to wait alone with his thoughts, he'd been driving himself crazy, worrying about Marcie and how she'd manage on her own in her condition. Abby's voice was like a lifeline.

He crossed to her in swift, sure strides. "You talked her out of it?"

"I talked her into listening to her common sense," Abby corrected. Whatever the negatives, she thought, the man's obvious love for his sister put him well into the plus column. "She's just hurt and angry over your last argument. Under all those smoldering emotions is a girl who is very grateful to you for all you've done and who has a great deal of respect for you.''

Amazement highlighted his features. They'd been arguing for what seemed like five endless years, he and Marcie. He'd almost become convinced his sister hated him. ''She said that?''

''What she said was that she didn't think, in your place, that she would have been able to make all the sacrifices that you'd made to get both of you where you are today. That chalks up to respect in my book.''

He took her hands in his. He didn't attempt to kid himself. If not for Abby, Marcie would have been gone by now. Even if his sister hadn't wanted to leave home, there was such a thing as stubborn pride. They both had it in spades. It was a family curse.

''Abby, I don't know how to thank you.''

Well, she did. ''Oh, there's one more thing.''

There were terms to go along with this. He should have realized there would be. Braced for the worst, Kyle asked, ''Yes?''

He looked, Abby thought, like someone waiting for a bomb to be detonated. She knew he was under a lot of stress; she remembered the article she'd read in the paper the other day about a thwarted takeover of his company. Her sister Anna had brought it to her attention, thinking she'd be interested.

''Marcie still wants you to be her birthing coach.''

It was a small price to pay, albeit an uncomfortable one, for having his sister remain at home. Relieved, resigned, Kyle nodded. ''And here I thought I could get out of it.'' He shrugged. ''Take the good with the bad, right?''

He just didn't get it, did he? "In case you don't know it, this is one of the good."

"If you say so." Kyle glanced toward the hall and the stairs beyond. There were still loose ends flapping around. "I want to go up and talk to Marcie." He looked at her. "Will you still be here when I come out? In case I need a mediator again," he added. It wasn't the only reason he wanted her to stay. Or even the major one. But it was a reason they could both accept.

They had unfinished business of a different sort to tend to.

Abby shrugged. "Unless the bus has taken to stopping at your door, I still need a ride back to the clinic and my car."

Reassured, Kyle started up the stairs. "Knew I did something right today."

THE EVENING TRAFFIC had thinned considerably, and the trip from his house to the clinic's parking lot was over all too soon. He could see the tall building, all its stories lit up, looming ahead. But he didn't want Abby to go just yet.

Purposely slowing, he missed the light at the corner. "I'd like to thank you properly for going out of your way like that."

Abby shrugged. "You threw the photographer out of the day care center. I'd say we're even."

That sounded far too much like a business negotiation to him. "Humor me. I don't like being on the receiving end and not reciprocating." The driver behind him beeped his horn. Only then did Kyle realize the light had turned green. He moved his foot back to the accelerator. "Why don't I drop you off at the clinic, you drive your car home, and then I can come by to take you to dinner?'' When she hesitated, he added quickly, ''I cleared the evening, anyway, and I'm not the type to sit around doing nothing.''

He was also, Abby thought, not the type to take no for an answer. Not that she was about to give it. But she couldn't resist saying, ''You could try reading a good book.''

Kyle shook his head.

''Too passive.'' He slanted a look at her, but couldn't see her expression. ''So, is that a no?''

It should have been, she thought, if she had any sense. He was giving her a way out, one she should take. Whatever was happening between them wasn't going to go anywhere. She didn't want it to.

Once burnt…

But she found herself shaking her head and saying, ''That's a suggestion.'' And then at the last minute, she hid behind a handy excuse. ''I really don't have time to fly to another restaurant.''

''No flying,'' he promised, then, glanced over at her, raising and lowering his eyebrows. ''Unless my company makes you light-headed. I thought we'd go somewhere local.'' A diner, if that's what it took to snare a little of her time. Or even takeout. ''What's your pleasure?'' he prodded. ''Quiet and intimate, or loud and rousing?''

Intimate wouldn't be a good idea. Intimate meant he could get another chance to kiss her. Last time he'd dissolved her knees—who knew what would go this time? ''Loud and rousing.''

The thrill of victory hummed through him just as boisterously as it had when he'd landed his first contract. ''You're on.''

MUTTERING UNDER HER BREATH, still dripping despite the rigorous toweling she'd given herself as she'd jumped out of the shower after only three minutes, Abby hurried into her bedroom.

There were technical articles with her name on them, piled precariously high beside an army of multicolored stick-on tabs, waiting to be read and annotated. Not to mention the dictations she had yet to make for Lisa to transcribe.

Any way she looked at it, she had a multitude of things to catch up on, not the least of which was peace and quiet. She couldn't remember when she'd had a real moment to herself. With all this waiting for her, there was no way she could justify going out tonight.

Except that she wanted to be with Kyle.

Abby frowned. She was running across quicksand, she warned herself as she struggled to reach the zipper at the back of her dress. A triumphant noise escaped her lips as she secured the tiny tongue and yanked the zipper up.

With a quick, appraising glance, Abby surveyed herself in the mirror. She smoothed out her dress along her hips, imagining his hands there instead of hers.

Stop it, warned the woman in the mirror. *You know what happens when you lead with your feelings instead of your mind. People like Drew happen.*

"Forewarned, forearmed," Abby replied to the reflection.

The woman in the mirror looked unconvinced.

The doorbell rang, and as her heart launched itself into her throat, Abby realized she wasn't forearmed at all. The woman in the mirror was right.

Telling herself not to be ridiculous, she hurried to the door and pulled it open.

The greeting on Kyle's lips faltered at the sight of her. How could something as simple as a basic black dress look so mouthwateringly sensational?

Suddenly, he wanted to tell her that the town was shut down in a power failure, that they would just have to stay home, light candles, make their own entertainment... And he knew just how to keep her amused.

You're behaving like a high school kid, Kyle chided himself. It was a matter of life catching up to him. In high school, he hadn't had time to be a kid.

"You look sensational." His glance lowered to her feet. "But I don't know about those shoes."

Abby looked down. She didn't see anything wrong with the matching black pumps and their three-inch heels. "What's wrong with my shoes?"

"They don't look suitable for dancing."

Her eyes widened. She'd just been thinking of food. "We're going dancing?"

It was a pleasant change and one he hoped she might enjoy. "I thought you wanted a rousing restaurant. Rousing means dancing to me." Maybe he'd read her wrong. "We can always go somewhere else."

It might be fun at that. Abby shook her head. "No, dancing is fine." As long as all the songs they played were fast and she didn't find herself lost in his arms, she added silently. Otherwise...

EVEN THOUGH it was a trendy new place, Abby had only heard about the Wandering I. But judging from the lineup around the block, she was probably the only one who hadn't wanted to go. There was no way they'd get in tonight, she thought.

Leaving his car for the valet to deal with, Kyle took her hand and wove his way to the front of the long line.

Sharp protests and words that had no place in polite society were flung their way.

Abby winced at a particularly colorful epithet. "I'm kind of new at this," she hissed into his ear, "but aren't we supposed to go to the end of the line?"

Kyle didn't even bother glancing back. "Everyone gets reviewed before they're approved or passed over. Approval's not a given, no matter how long you wait." Time was always of the essence. "I figured we'd save some time and find out now if we're in or not."

Something within Abby froze as they approached the head of the line. Drew had made her sensitive to people who wanted to use her family name to open doors for them. She knew why they'd come here. It was a feeling of power to be able to walk past the throngs. Kyle was going to use her to get into the club.

She would put a stop to it now. Halting, Abby tugged on Kyle's hand just as they reached the tall, muscular doorman who guarded the red rope before him as if it were the boundary between heaven and hell.

Surprised, Kyle looked over his shoulder at her. It was too noisy for a conversation, but he silently raised his brow.

Before she could tell him she wanted to leave, the bouncer turned in their direction. Almost immediately, the critical scowl on his wide, youthful face disappeared. The smile that replaced it almost made him look genial. "Hey, Mr. Mac, how's it going?"

"Great, Jefferson." He inclined his head toward Abby. "The lady and I would like to—"

"Say no more. You're in, man." With a flourish, Jefferson unhooked the rope and held it up high, letting them pass. His hand shot out, making contact with the chest of the man behind Abby who was trying to elbow his way in, as well. "Wait your turn," Jefferson growled.

Stunned, Abby followed Kyle in wordlessly. Once inside, she found herself almost wedged against him by the crowd. "You know him?"

Kyle lowered his head and spoke into her ear. "His younger brother goes to this center for underprivileged kids. I gave a talk there the other month. Plus some free computers. Figured they'd like those better than listening to some 'rich dude' talk. Jefferson happened to be there at the same time." There was more to it than that, but he felt elaborating would only make him look as if he were on an ego trip. It was enough that doing an occasional good deed created a warm feeling within him. Almost as warm as the feeling of having her close this way… "Told me if I was ever in the area—" The rest of his sentence was swallowed up by the noise.

"You do get around," she murmured to herself.

"What?" Shaking his head, he indicated his ear.

Abby cupped her hand around her mouth. "Nothing. How do we hear ourselves think in this place?"

He grinned. "We don't. They tell me that's part of the fun." Looking around, he saw a couple of free tables beyond the dance floor. "Looks like the dining area's divided into two sections—deafening noise and not-so-deafening noise." Kyle looked at her. "What's your preference?"

"Not-so-deafening." She figured she was still going to go hoarse within the hour.

"Good choice." His hand tightening around hers, he led the way to the rear. "Your word is my command."

THE WALL OF NOISE was only slightly muted on this side of the room. It gave him the opportunity to study Abby in between fitful attempts at conversation over the slightly wobbly round table. He leaned over it now to make himself heard without shouting. ''Everything to your liking?''

Maybe it was Abby's imagination, but his eyes seemed to tease her as he asked the question. Was it himself or the club in general that he was referring to? ''Excuse me?''

Kyle nodded at her plate. For the most part, she'd been pushing her food around on it, eating sparingly. He made the logical assumption. ''We can send it back if you'd rather have something else.''

It took her a moment to process his words. When she did, she drew the plate closer to her.

''Oh, no, this is fine. As a matter of fact, the food's remarkably good for a place that seems predominantly devoted to packing as many bodies as humanly possible onto the dance floor and then having them struggle in some form of a mating ritual.''

The description made him grin. Kyle turned around to look himself. ''They do seem to be having a good time, don't they.'' And he had waited long enough to become part of it. ''Since you don't seem to be that interested in eating, can I interest you in engaging in that mating ritual?''

The music played by the live band, who were on a stage suspended above the center of the crowd, throbbed and vibrated throughout her body. It was impossible to ignore and difficult to resist.

A little, she realized, like the man sitting opposite her. Taking a deep breath, knowing she was about to jump into deeper waters, Abby nodded. ''I'd love to dance with you.''

Kyle was already on his feet. He held out his hand to her. "Well then, what are we waiting for?"

A last-minute reprieve from the governor before I get myself even more tangled up, Abby thought, even as she let him wrap his hand around hers.

Kyle led her the short distance onto the floor, and they took their places at the perimeter. Within seconds, they were engulfed by the rhythm, made one with the music. And with each other. As they moved to the almost primitive beat, their bodies brushed up against each other like two pieces of flint, promising the birth of fire.

Abby's entire body was pounding wildly by the time the song ended. Seamlessly, another song began, much slower, bringing them within a breath of each other.

As Kyle took her into his arms, he tucked her hand into his and pressed it against his shoulder. Closing his eyes, he leaned his cheek against her hair. The scent he breathed in gently conquered the tangle of perfume and cologne drifting on the air around them. It filled his senses, quickened his appetite. And made his desire for her border on sweet agony.

Gradually, he became aware of something else, and wondered about it. "You're supposed to be enjoying yourself," he whispered against her ear.

Abby tried not to shiver as his breath skimmed along her neck. Tried not to let herself imagine what being alone with him would be like. She forced herself to look up at him. Anything else would have been cowardly.

"I am."

The hell she was. "Then why are you so rigid?"

The shrug was casual. "Just good posture."

His laugh rumbled in his chest, teasing her. "West Point Cadets are less rigid."

"They've relaxed the requirements," she murmured back.

He couldn't make himself believe that she was somehow afraid of him. The only fear he ever inspired was within the world of computer technology, not on the dance floor. There had to be another reason for the way she was acting. "Relax. That's right," he coaxed. "Let the music take you."

She moistened her lips, but it didn't seem to help. "It's not the music I'm worried about."

He drew his head back to look down into her eyes, searching for things she wasn't telling him. What he saw made him realize that she was vulnerable. Something protective stirred within him.

"It shouldn't be me you're worried about, either." The smile on his lips was meant to put her at ease. "I would have thought that for someone like you, this would be old hat."

It had been a long time since she'd frequented a place like this. Her college years, to be precise. "The hat's been in a closet a very long time."

There was no reason for her to lie, and she didn't strike him as a woman who'd be coy. There was only one conclusion. "Are all the men in your life blind?"

Though she tried to stop it, pleasure flared deep within her at the compliment. "The men in my life are all married. Husbands to my patients," she explained when he continued looking at her, an incredulous expression in his eyes. "Work takes up most of my time. I don't get out much."

He'd seen her picture in the paper once, but now that he thought of it, it had been in connection with the clinic—some charity function she was attending. Still, she had to have more of a social life than she was owning up to. "I find that very difficult to wrap my mind around."

There was no room in her life for casual, or even not-so-casual, dating. She'd seen to that. "I have a thriving practice and wall-to-wall patients. Believe it."

The sudden flash just to the right of Abby abruptly ended the conversation and temporarily blinded her. A sliver of uncertainty pricked her, and she tightened her grip on Kyle. "What was that?"

But Kyle wasn't answering her. She could hear him shouting at someone, and her vision slowly began to clear. Shapes careened in front of her—and then she saw the camera.

"Out recreating while your brothers are procreating, eh, Abby?" The photographer aimed his camera at them, laughing at his own cleverness. "One more, Abby. This time drape yourself over McDermott again. If it weren't for the little bastard, this would be on the front page next week."

Kyle pushed Abby behind him, blocking her with his body. The fighter within her took exception; the weary woman was grateful.

"I said, get the hell away from her." There was something about the photographer pushing his camera at Abby that made Kyle become fiercely protective. He could see himself smashing his fist into the man's square face.

"Hey, free country, McDermott. You and she don't own it yet. I paid my way in just like everyone else." He kept snapping away as he spoke, undoubtedly hop-ing there would be something salable in the developed film. "I've got every right to be here."

As he lifted his camera higher to focus it, Kyle pulled

it away from him and tossed it to the ground. The glass lens shattered.

Incensed, the man shrieked his outrage. "What the hell did you do that for?"

As if merging into one consciousness, the crowd had grown quieter, encircling the three players.

Kyle kicked the camera aside, out of the photographer's reach. "I said to leave her alone."

The man glared at him. "She doesn't want her picture taken, she shouldn't be in places like this." Scurrying like a rodent, he managed to scoop up his camera. The last bits of glass rained down on his arm. His dark eyes narrowed into malevolent pinpricks. "You freakin' bastard, you broke my camera! I'll sue you!"

The man dropped the camera and charged at Kyle, fists flying. But Kyle was ready for him.

"Well, if you're going to sue me, I might as well get some enjoyment out of this," he said as his fist connected with the man's jaw, sending him flying to the floor. Ignoring the howls of pain, Kyle turned to Abby. "I think we should have picked intimate and quiet instead. Ready to go?"

Abby nodded. Passing their table, Kyle tossed several large bills down, covering the meal and drinks as well as any damages they might have incurred.

It was only after he'd slipped his arm protectively around her that Abby noticed Kyle's knuckles were bleeding.

CHAPTER TWELVE

"LET ME LOOK at your knuckles." Annoyed that he'd gotten hurt because of her, Abby tried to examine the extent of the damage to his hand.

Kyle didn't want her making a fuss over it, especially not when he was trying to get her out of here before the obnoxious photographer could scramble to his feet and give chase. Kyle continued to usher her through the crowd.

"It's nothing," he almost growled. He glanced over his shoulder, but the crowd had closed ranks behind him. The photographer was nowhere to be seen. Good.

The air outside felt cool after the hot press of bodies inside. Kyle drew in a deep breath, on his guard until he could get her inside the safety of his car.

"Hey, Mr. Mac," the bouncer called to him, a bemused expression across his wide features, "you and the lady leaving so soon?" Without looking, he shifted, blocking a couple who were trying to get by him. They slunk back into line.

Kyle shrugged casually. "Evening's young. Places to go, things to see."

The bouncer leaned over to get a better view of Abby. His grin was huge when he straightened again. He winked broadly at Kyle. "I got your message."

"And you," Abby said firmly, taking hold of Kyle's hand the moment they were clear of the front entrance, "should get mine." Quickly, she examined his knuckles. Even by streetlight, she could see that they were scraped and beginning to show signs of swelling and bruising. The other man must have a chin made out of corrugated metal, she thought. A flicker of guilt mixed with concern as she glanced up at him. "This is the part they never tell you about in all those action movies. Punching someone really messes up your hand."

Granted, his knuckles stung, but it was well worth it, Kyle thought. He hadn't liked the photographer's attitude toward Abby. The man had treated her as if she were a commodity.

Very deliberately, Kyle drew his hand out of hers and slid it into his pocket. "Guess I'll just have to give up moonlighting as a hand model. Here—" He gave his ticket to the valet and watched the man hurry off, his blond ponytail bouncing each time his feet made contact with the pavement.

Abby wasn't about to be put off. "When you take me home, I want you to come inside."

The smile on his face was so sexy, Abby felt her breath momentarily hitch in her throat.

"Why, Abby, this is so sudden."

The man was obviously good at diversions. But she was better at being single-minded. "That could get ugly," Abby said, pointing to the hand he still hid in his pocket. "I want to make sure there's no infection."

"Yes, Doc."

His meek manner didn't fool her for a minute. She doubted that Kyle McDermott had known a meek, submissive moment in his life.

"How do you put up with it?" His question broke into her thoughts. "The photographers, the people prying into your affairs?"

"Well, when I don't have someone coming to my
rescue—" she glanced at him, smiling "—I try to ignore it. It isn't normally so bad, but this thing with the
mystery baby has caused a major flare-up. It'll die down
again soon enough. I hope." She paused. "To be honest, when it gets bad like this, I've flirted with the idea
of disappearing, like Jake…"

Kyle thought a second before the identity became
clear to him. He'd been doing some reading up on the
Maitlands. "Your brother, right?"

Abby nodded, moving to the side as a couple leaving
the club passed them.

"He avoids all public attention," she said, then
added under her breath, "along with most family contact." But Jake's way wasn't hers. "My heart is here,
though, with my work." She pressed her lips together,
looking at Kyle again. "Does that sound very corny?"

"No, not corny. I'm beginning to think that sounds
very 'you.'"

Abby found herself smiling as the valet pulled up.

SHE BROUGHT HIM into a dining room that seemed remarkably informal, given Abby's social position. There
was no outright show of wealth. The table and chairs
were light pine, tasteful, but chosen mostly with an eye
to comfort, Kyle thought.

Abby made him sit down like a child while she went
to the medicine cabinet and got out the items she
needed. Kyle thought of brushing her off. He'd suffered
injuries in his time that were a hell of a lot worse than
scraped knuckles. But there was something about having her minister to him that he found oddly appealing.
Soothing and arousing at the same time. It wouldn't hurt
to let her do it a little longer.

She brought a small basin filled with warm, sudsy water and made him soak his hand in it. The contact stung, but he tried to keep the fact from registering on his face.

Abby saw his eyes water a little. The man was determined to behave like a typical male, stoically enduring pain without showing it. She wondered what other kind of pain he'd endured. Had there been someone in his life, someone who'd broken his heart and left?

His past love life was none of her business, she told herself, but it was hard not to think about romance, when he was here, so close to her.

"That's twice in one day," Abby said out loud, giving voice to her thoughts. Gently, she dried his hand, wiping it slowly as if it belonged to a small boy, instead of a man who made her blood heat just by the way he looked at her.

Kyle's reaction was hardly that of a child. The gentler she was, the more she stirred him, sending his mind to places he hadn't thought to visit. He struggled to come to grips with the restlessness that traveled through him. But it was growing rather than shrinking. And her perfume was partially to blame. Her perfume and the way her breasts seductively rose and fell with every breath she took.

She was making his mouth turn to cotton. "What, that you've made my heart stop by being so close?"

The comment, with its underpinning of raw sexuality, caught her off guard. She avoided his eyes as she continued working.

"No, that you've come to my rescue." She finished drying his hand and ventured a glance at his face, ordering herself not to reveal her true feelings. "Maybe I should hire you to be my bodyguard."

The smile was slow, sensual. "You couldn't afford to pay me."

In an attempt to remove himself from temptation, Kyle drew his hand away from hers, though he had to admit that part of him enjoyed having her fuss over him. It was a completely new experience. One he could get used to, if he allowed himself.

The muted lights from the Tiffany lamp overhead played off her hair, and he had to curb the desire to run his fingers through it. "However, I could be persuaded to volunteer."

Trying to keep her mind on what she was doing, Abby firmly took his hand in hers again. She held it as if it were a paw belonging to a skittish pet and carefully dabbed the reddened area with peroxide. "You already have. Volunteered," she added when he made no comment.

The degree to which he wanted her astounded him. Kyle moved aside the supplies she'd laid out on the table. When she raised her eyes questioningly to his, he said, "You know, if you really want to play doctor, I have a better idea how to go about it."

He slipped his hands around hers and rose to his feet, taking her with him.

There went her heart again, she thought. This time it felt as if it were hiccuping, skipping beats and then rushing to make up the difference. She used the last of her breath to ask, "How better?"

The softly whispered question just served to excite him even more. "This better." Bending his head, he showed her. He kissed her. Kissed her the way he'd been wanting to all evening. The way he'd been wanting to ever since he first saw her raise her chin in her reception area as if to take him on.

This time, he knew what was coming, and was prepared.

But memory had not served him well, he discovered. He didn't remember this burning hunger, this desire that rose up unchecked within him.

Kyle groaned, knowing he was lost. He cupped her chin with his hand and tilted her head back just a little.

Just enough.

The kiss deepened.

And he felt himself drowning. His last lucid thought was that he must take her with him.

Completely forgetting that his right hand was still damp from the peroxide Abby had poured over it, Kyle drew her into his arms and held her tightly against him as he kissed her over and over. Everything seemed to swirl around him, and he was lost in a sea of emotions, swept away before his surprise could even begin to register.

A moan lingered in Abby's throat, echoing in her brain. Her thoughts were in a state of utter chaos as she drove her fingers into his hair, eager for the very feel of him. She'd had no idea how needy she had been until he'd opened this door for her.

Her body vibrated in silent supplication. Pleading. Demanding. Her breathing quickened, and the room began to swirl around her.

When his mouth continued to draw the very life out of her, offering her ecstasy in return, there was no hesitancy on her part. She gave, and took. And hoped that reason would never return.

At last she drew her head back, her eyes vaguely unfocused, and gazed up at him. "So far, so good." She had to stop to draw in enough breath to continue. "What else did you have in mind?"

Kyle looked as disoriented as she felt. "I'm more of a hands-on man than a lecturer."

Anticipation enveloped her body with whispered promises. "Then show me."

His eyes grew dusky. "I intend to."

His words vibrated along her throat as he pressed a kiss there, followed by an army of others that laid siege to her cheeks, her chin, her eyelids. Abby's head dropped back, and she had to force herself to focus.

Wondrous as all this was to experience, she couldn't allow herself to be passive. She had to drag him into this ring of fire he was creating, bring him in with her until they were both burning.

As if gunpowder had exploded in her veins, Abby launched her assault, her mouth savaging his lips, his throat, her teeth just barely skimming the point of his chin as her tongue flicked over it. When she heard him moan, the rush she felt fueled her, pushing her on. She was his equal in every way. His benevolent jailer, his willing prisoner, just as he was hers.

If he wasn't careful, Kyle realized, she was going to wind up doing all the work—all the pleasuring. Much as he enjoyed what she was doing and the effects it was having on his body, he refused to allow his lovemaking to be one-sided. For the life of him, he had never been able to understand a man who derived pleasure solely from receiving, when the greatest satisfaction came from giving.

With hands that felt as if they were shaking, he reached behind her and slowly worked down the zipper of her dress. His eyes held hers. Watching.

In his mind, or at least the part that was still coherent, Kyle held his breath, waiting for her reaction. Waiting to detect the slightest bit of hesitancy on her part. Intoxicated with her or not, he wasn't about to take what wasn't being given.

But it took only a moment for him to realize that it *was* being given. She was giving herself to him, and it was a gift of the highest magnitude.

He was humbled. He was eager.

Abby shivered as the dress fell from her shoulders. She held her breath in anticipation of what was to follow, warning herself not to set her expectations too high.

But it was too late. They *were* high. And he was up to them.

She felt his hands on her a moment before he touched her. The gentleness surprised her. And made her want to cry. The passion in his eyes made her think that he would be less than tender, less than patient.

But she was wrong. He was both.

And more.

Her head spun as he cupped her breasts, his thumbs slowly working their way beneath the lacy fabric of her bra until it was skin against skin. She was enflamed even as she shivered. Waiting for more.

Every movement was slow, languid. He was making her crazy. He was making her body scream for more.

Urgency pumped through her veins, and she unhooked his pants at the same moment that the clasp at her back came free, releasing her taut breasts.

In choppy, jagged movements, she pulled the zipper of his pants just as Kyle slowly slid the bra straps from her shoulders. The garment hung loose about her arms, leaving her uncovered by anything but his deep gaze. And then his hands. Her heart was racing.

His breathing became audible to her.

Her hands slipped beneath the waistband of his briefs,

and she felt his muscles tighten as she slid the material over firm, smooth hips, the evidence of his desire pressing against her.

He stepped out of his shoes, and then out of the trousers, even as his fingers hooked the fallen bra straps and sent the lacy garment fluttering to the floor. Trousers and dress, briefs and bra were left to commune as he drew her to him.

Kyle had thought his body was beyond growing any hotter. He realized now that he'd miscalculated. It was happening even now as he looked at her.

She had on a creamy scrap of silk that someone, on a whim, had called underwear. And nothing else. Kyle felt everything tightening within him like the strings of a violin pulled taut.

At any other time, the fact that he was wearing only his shirt would have seemed incredibly sexy to Abby. But now it represented the last barrier that kept him from her.

Her breath caught in her throat as she felt his fingers moving gently down her belly. Swallowing a gasp, she yanked the shirt off his shoulders, sending one button into oblivion before she remembered to undo the rest. His mouth was grazing along her shoulders, and then her breasts, even as his fingers delved deeper, sending her to a mind-numbing place where her blood pumped hot and wild sensations mingled with a bevy of blinding lights.

Her breath was ragged, labored as her head dropped back again. He'd brought her to a peak, then pushed her up and over before she could realize what he was doing.

Wonder filled her eyes as she stared at him, pupils

unfocused. Kyle had never seen anything so simple and yet so beautiful in his life.

Lifting her into his arms, he carried her to the sofa. The bedroom seemed half a continent away, in a land he had no strength to seek out. All he wanted was to lose himself in her, in the scent, the feel, the music of her. If there was any strength within him, he wanted to reserve it for her. To make love with her until eternity took them as its own.

Freeing her from the last silky barrier, Kyle eased Abby down onto the sofa. Sliding in beside her, he set about his exploration, charting routes to secret places that thrilled him, as one by one they revealed themselves to him.

Moaning, Abby arched against him, absorbing the feel of his hand, his lips. Wanting more. Needing more.

He was making her body throb, making her want so badly that she could barely hold her cries in check. Desperately, she wanted their joining to happen. Now. She clutched at his shoulders, trying to drag him back up to her, but her fingers were weak. All of her was weak. And growing weaker even as the rapture grew.

She couldn't catch hold of a thought. Everything was swirling around her. The room, sensations. Him. She felt his lips, his teeth, his tongue brand her, drive her crazy.

Explosions racked her body as his tongue thrust, first slowly, then faster and faster, setting her inner core on fire. Her pulse scrambling, she could feel herself growing closer and closer to the moment. She could only reach for him and hope to make contact. All thought of reciprocation left her. She didn't know how to do this, didn't know how to make a man want to beg. The way she wanted to.

"If you don't come up here now," she warned hoarsely, "I can't be held accountable for my actions."

She felt his body slide tantalizingly over hers, radiating heat. A teasing smile was on his lips when she finally focused on the face hovering over hers.

"Was there something you wanted to take up with me?" he asked.

"Yes." A laugh came from deep within her, then his mouth covered hers.

Her legs opened for Kyle, and he slid inside her, surrendering to the hunger that all but consumed him. He felt her muscles tighten around him, felt the blood rushing through his body, leaving him light-headed.

The rhythm, born from urgency, increased in tempo until it had them both firmly in its grip, spinning them mindlessly to completion.

Abby felt herself drift back to consciousness, and it was as if a beautiful silken blanket floated down from the sky, gently draping her, wrapping her in the fragile beauty of the moment.

Tightening her arms around Kyle, she desperately sought to hold on to the glow. This had to be euphoria, she thought. And if it wasn't, then she didn't have a clue what euphoria really meant.

Her heart was still slamming against her rib cage, but she didn't care. Even if this was her last moment on earth, it had been worth it.

She wasn't saying anything, but Kyle could feel her breath grazing his shoulder. Concern nudged away the shimmering web of contentment that enveloped him. He shifted his head until his face was a scant half-inch from hers. "Am I hurting you?" he asked.

"I don't know." She tried to rouse herself, but failed.

She didn't want to move. Ever. "I think I just had an out-of-body experience."

Concern melted into a smile. She was delectable like this. "Too bad, because I was in mine, and I wouldn't have missed it for the world." Pivoting himself on his elbows, unwilling to break the union just yet, he rose slightly above her and framed her face between his hands. "You, lady, are something else."

Good something else or...? Had she disappointed him somehow? Toward the end, all she had been able to do was hang on. "What?" she asked hoarsely. "What else?"

He moved his head slowly from side to side. "I don't know." He ran the tip of his finger along the hollow of her throat and watched the pulse there come to life. "I don't think they've created a word for it yet."

Kyle rolled off and gathered her to him in one smooth movement. It had been a long time since he'd made love with a woman, and even longer since it had come about because of need rather than simply desire born of the moment. He couldn't remember ever wanting anyone like this. Nor could he remember ever feeling sated and vaguely hungry at the same time.

He kissed her temple, a sweetness mingling with nascent desire. "You were magnificent."

Her mouth curved slightly. Her body was still tingling. "You weren't half bad yourself."

He arched an eyebrow. "Half bad?"

"*Weren't* half bad," she corrected. "You missed the important word."

"*Weren't* half bad," he echoed. "That means not half good." He frowned thoughtfully, then sighed. "I guess we're just going to have to do it all over again so you can realize how wrong you are."

Her eyes widened even though she was trying to play along. ''Again?''

Could he make love with her again so soon? Drew had told her that any man's claim to more than once a night was sheer bragging and nothing more. There had been no one before Drew, so she had believed him.

There was laughter in Kyle's eyes at her reaction. And desire. ''Again.''

Abby turned her body toward him, excitement and anticipation stirring her. ''Threats, threats, threats...'' Her mouth curved around the last word as it melted against his.

CHAPTER THIRTEEN

MORNING WHISPERED at the curtains, slipping in softly, nudging Kyle awake. He resisted as long as he could before opening his eyes. The surprise of finding Abby beside him, nestled against the curve of his body, faded even as it registered.

So, he hadn't dreamed it. The night of wild passion and phenomenal acrobatics had been real. The wonder of it returned, coaxing a smile from him.

Whoever said that still waters ran deep had to have had Abby Maitland in mind.

He wanted to remain like this forever, but reality intruded. Though the hour was early, he had to get going. He had a meeting at nine-thirty, and preparations to make before then.

Kyle couldn't resist pressing a kiss to Abby's bare shoulder. She murmured something in her sleep, rousing. Smiling. And making his blood rush all over again.

When she opened her eyes to him, it was all he could do not to take her into his arms again. He couldn't recall ever feeling this strongly about a woman before.

He pushed back a strand of her hair, gently tucking it behind her ear. He'd asked before, but he still didn't understand. "How is it that you're not involved with anyone?"

The delicious feeling that had held her in its embrace when she woke up faded. Suspicion came on stealthy feet, cracking the door open a fraction. Peering in. Ushering in a cold draft in its wake.

"Why?"

Words failed him. Instead, he gave a slight shake of his head. "You take my breath away, Abby. I just wondered…"

The meaning behind his question slammed into her. "You think I'd be like this with anyone? *Do* this with anyone? Just hop into bed with them after rubbing peroxide on knuckles they skinned for me?" Is that what he really thought of her? She could feel tears beginning to form, and blinked hard to keep them back. "At the risk of sounding horribly unsophisticated, I don't sleep around."

Hurt and anger tore holes into the contentment that had been blanketing her. Bent on blind retreat, Abby abruptly turned from him and sat up, swinging her legs out of bed.

"Abby, I didn't—"

But she was already getting up. Stunned, he caught her by the shoulder, stopping her. Gently, but firmly, Kyle held her in place and then made her turn around again to face him.

"Abby, I didn't mean to make it sound like that. I just can't believe that no one's ever—"

She didn't want to hear him ask it. Couldn't bear to hear him say it. With bravado, she held his eyes with hers. "Someone has."

"Oh." Of course there had to have been someone. Then why was there such a sinking feeling in his chest, in his stomach? A sinking feeling that there had been someone in her life who had meant something to her. Maybe it was because, secretly, he hadn't wanted there to be.

She couldn't read his expression, couldn't see if the news meant something, or less than nothing. Or if it was relief he felt at not being the only one in her life. He was probably afraid she'd put too much significance on their night of lovemaking. Men had rational, cool thoughts once their bodies had ceased heating.

"The price was too high."

He didn't follow. "Price?"

Maybe it was the memory of Drew that did it. Made her need someone to protect her, if only for a moment. Very slowly, she allowed herself to be taken back into Kyle's arms.

"He wanted my name," she said. "Actually, the connections my name could bring him—and my money."

She couldn't keep the frown from her voice, or from her lips, any more than she could keep the hurt from her soul at the very memory of it all. It was three years in her past, yet it still hurt like tiny needles embedded under the skin.

"In exchange, he figured he'd turn my head with flattery and make love to me whenever I began to doubt his intentions. After a while, it became apparent that it wasn't humanly possible to make love that often." She looked at Kyle. "I told him I didn't want to be used. The jig, as they say, was up, and he went his way." Her mouth hardened. "But not before selling a particularly nasty piece to one of the tabloids."

He understood now. Understood and discovered that he had a sudden urge to pummel a nameless, faceless man into the ground. "And you've been gun-shy ever since."

She shrugged carelessly, her shoulder moving against his bare chest. It sent tiny missiles of sensation through him. "My work keeps me busy."

He knew better. Very lightly, he began a trail of tiny kisses up along her shoulder to her neck. "Your work keeps you hidden. It's a nice escape. Trouble is, if you're not careful, it has a way of swallowing you up."

Abby drew back her head, trying to blanket the smoldering feelings he was fanning into wakefulness. "This from a man who lives and breathes work."

"This from a man who lives and breathes work," he echoed. He tugged away the sheet she held against her breasts and softly kissed the tender flesh there. "Who better?" Damn, if he was late for the meeting, what could they do? It was *his* meeting. "I'm just now beginning to see the error of my ways."

God, but he was making it hard to think, to focus. Any second now, he was going to reduce her to a puddle of needs and desires. Again.

"Marcie should be the one who makes you see that," Abby managed to say, although she was no longer certain of the thread of her conversation. "She needs you, you know. For emotional support more than for financial."

"I've been there all along." When Abby moved her head back to look at him with eyes that were just the slightest bit dazed, he relented the point he was trying to drive home. "Okay, maybe not as much in body as in spirit, but I've told her..."

If he didn't stop, she was going to forget not just the direction of her argument, but her name, rank and serial number, as well. "She doesn't want you telling her. She wants your time, your attention. There's...there's a difference."

Her labored breathing was turning him on. "You've got a good heart, Abby." He covered her breast with his palm, cupping her. "And I think I hear it calling to me again."

"You wish."

The sexy smile on his lips curled upward like smoke. "You're right. I wish."

"Me, too," she murmured against his mouth, giving up the fight she hadn't even wanted to win.

"FLOWERS FOR Dr. Maitland. Sign here, please."

Dana thought the delivery man looked impatient to be gone. It was a little after five in the afternoon, and it was obvious that he wanted to knock off for the day.

On her way out after a quick visit, she paused to smell the arrangement of yellow roses and baby's breath. Not the usual sort of gift to come into an obstetrician's office.

She saw Abby take out the note, read it. And smile. Her curiosity was aroused.

"Someone saying thank-you?" she prodded. Abby had brought more than her share of babies into the world, and gifts were often sent in thanks for the extra mile she would go.

"In a manner of speaking."

Dana raised a brow at the enigmatic answer. "Oh?" She reached for the card in Abby's hands, but Abby pulled it away before she could get it. "Who?" And then she knew. Or at least suspected. "Not Kyle McDermott."

"Would that make you happy? Okay, not Kyle McDermott."

Dana had her answer. "It is. It *is* Kyle McDermott."

"Dana, so help me, if you squeal and invite me over for a slumber party, I may have to terminate our friendship."

"Sometimes, Abby, you're just no fun." Dana pretended to pout, then added, "but as long as Kyle thinks you are, it really doesn't matter what I think, does it? He certainly has nice taste." Her tone was teasing. "But we already know that, don't we?"

"I have a lecture to deliver."

A likely story. But Dana could take a hint—when it was shoved at her. "To anyone I know?"

"Katie was tapped to take over the birthing class at the last minute because Allison came down with the flu. She's desperate, so I promised I'd stop by to help." Pushing her purse up her arm, she locked the door.

"You're just doing that so you won't have to answer my questions, aren't you?"

"See, you don't need me," Abby pointed out. "You're answering your own questions now. Pretty soon, you'll be carrying on a regular conversation." With that, she hurried off to the elevator.

Thinking of the roses, Abby smiled all over again. Just when she thought that perhaps he was trying to avoid her... Just goes to show, she thought, you never knew with a man. They were impossible creatures to read.

Getting on the elevator, she pressed the button for the ground floor.

She found herself smiling. And humming.

No matter how much she told herself that she was simply indulging in a fling, that nothing serious was going to come of her seeing Kyle—if indeed she continued to see him—Abby knew that she was not just passively watching events take place. Her feelings were swiftly becoming invested—if they hadn't already been commandeered.

Abby sighed. There was no getting away from it. She

wasn't the kind who knew how to have a fling, who could dance lightly through the lovemaking and the laughter, and just leave her heart out of it. Her heart was very much a part of everything she did, whether it was ministering to patients who looked to her for advice and guidance, or kissing a dark-haired man with eyes like heaven and a mouth that tasted of sin.

Especially the latter, she thought.

Her heart might be involved, but by no means did that mean that his was. Abby's smile grew. Abby wasn't sure just what of him was invested in this, beyond the obvious.

She would have been suspicious, she reminded herself as she watched a mother and her twin sons get off the elevator, if he had moved in on her too fast. She'd been swept off her feet once, and had landed unceremoniously on her posterior.

But her caution didn't change the fact that she greeted each day with a wee bit more enthusiasm than was her custom, hoping to see Kyle again. It had been several days now and she'd almost given up hope, thinking she had to have slipped his mind. Until the flowers arrived.

The note said he'd been too busy to call. But not too busy to think.

She liked the implications. The man was smooth.

And tonight, she thought, she was going to see that smooth man under fire. Tonight's birthing class was the one he and Marcie were enrolled in.

This, she told herself as she got off the elevator, promised to be interesting.

THE BIRTHING CLASS was in a large room reserved for social gatherings at the clinic. It had a festive look that did a great deal to dispel unease, the kind that first-time fathers-to-be brought with them when faced with all this "female mumbo jumbo," as one man in the class had put it.

Right now, it was littered with colorful blankets, large pillows and larger women, all on the floor in the throes of prenatal exercises.

As with every session, Katie was having them practice their breathing exercises, striving to make them second nature.

Kyle and Marcie were in the second row, third from the end. He was kneeling behind her, holding her slightly propped up on the pillow, coaching.

Standing off to the side, Abby indulged herself for a moment and watched them. Watched him.

He looked, she thought, like a duck not just out of water, but stuck in the middle of the desert without a compass or a prayer of finding a puddle to paddle in again. It wasn't so much his expression that gave him away. To his credit, he appeared stoic.

His expression was the kind she was sure he put on every time he confronted a challenging board meeting. Underneath that calm exterior was a cauldron of emotions she was willing to bet, all of them desperately urging him to flee.

It was his eyes that gave him away.

Since when have you become such an expert on Kyle McDermott? One coupling does not an authority make, she told herself.

But she had a feeling, a very strong feeling, that she was right. She just *sensed* it.

Slow down, Abby warned herself. What had happened to her being leery?

But had she been leery or paranoid? She didn't know anymore, but the lines were becoming blurred. She was so tempted to trust with her heart, but it had been her heart that had betrayed her last time. Her heart had made her believe things to be different than they were. Were they different now? Could she trust Kyle not to hurt her? To be exactly what he seemed? Or were there pitfalls she wasn't aware of, pitfalls she was blind to because all she could do was think about their night of lovemaking?

Fear of being too trusting dueled with her desire for a normal relationship. A relationship that held the promise of a prize at the end of it.

Her head was beginning to ache—

"Dr. Maitland?"

Abby heard her name, followed by Katie's slight clearing of her throat, and realized that the nurse was trying to get her attention. For how long? Abby wondered. She offered her friend an apologetic smile.

"Would you care to begin?" Katie prodded gently. The question in her eyes was barely hidden.

Katie was going to grill her the first chance she got, Abby thought. She tried to recover as best she could. "I was just looking at all these parents-to-be and thinking how lucky they are."

A man in the back groaned. The voice was too high to be Kyle's.

Leaning back against the table with its visual aids, Abby addressed her audience. "No, really, this is a miracle that you're all about to be part of."

Someone laughed nervously. "Pretty messy miracle," a man near the front muttered under his breath, but Abby managed to hear him.

"Messy, yes, and a little inconvenient—sometimes a lot," she amended before any of the pregnant women in the room could contradict her. "But everything worth having involves some inconvenience just to make the prize sweeter once you get it."

Pausing, Abby looked slowly around the room at the outward signs of love between the members of the various couples. Kyle's situation made her wonder how many more stand-in fathers were in the group. She hoped there were none. In her heart, she supposed that she secretly agreed with Kyle. If possible, a baby deserved to have both its mother and father at the advent of its birth.

But the world was far from a perfect place, and having a loving uncle smooth the way wasn't a bad thing.

She laced her hands before her. "I'm here to answer all your questions and to get you as comfortable with this whole process as I can."

Marcie spoke up. "Nothing short of a miracle is going to get me comfortable." With Kyle helping, she struggled into another position.

Marcie could do a lot worse than having a brother like Kyle in her life, Abby thought, watching. Approving.

"And a miracle you'll have," Abby promised with enthusiasm. No matter how many deliveries she attended, she felt there was something wondrous about each one. "A miracle to treasure, to hold for a very little while before it becomes old enough to tell you that he or she can do it by themselves, Mommy." Her grin was quick, infectious. "You may not think it now, but you're going to look back at this someday and sigh wistfully."

The soft murmur of voices told her that they didn't all agree with her prediction.

"Spoken like a woman who doesn't have any kids getting underfoot," someone quipped.

If he hadn't known any better, Kyle would have thought he just imagined it. A fleeting glimmer of hurt that came and went before a breath was completed. But it had been there, in her eyes, for a single heartbeat. She wanted children, he realized. And it probably killed her to bring so many into the world, none of them hers.

Why wasn't she married? Sure, she'd told him about that ass who had tried to use her, but there had to have been someone else.

The thought that there might not have been made him feel strangely humble and slightly bewildered. He couldn't decide if that was a good thing or bad, but he knew he wouldn't trade what had happened between them for any amount of share-splitting in the world.

"No, I don't," she said lightly. "You people keep me too busy to have a social life." Then she held up a hand when someone began to say something on the subject. "But I'm here to help *you,* not me." Though there was a smile on her face, there was a definite No Trespassing tone in her voice. She looked around again, signaling a new round. "Okay, let's get on with this, shall we?"

In simple, easy-to-understand terms, Abby reviewed procedures, fielded questions, and agreed to forego the video she'd brought with her when the two men up front turned a vivid shade of green as the opening credits began to roll. Instead, she discussed, as honestly as she could in the space of time they had, the very real fears plaguing the women and men gathered before her.

During the course of the meeting, she noticed that Kyle said nothing, asked nothing. He merely sat back and studied her thoughtfully.

Though he uttered not a sound, he made her lose her train of thought more than once, just by being there.

And looking like every fantasy she'd ever had in the middle of a cold, dark, lonely night.

The class ran over, but no one seemed to mind. At the end, when it finally broke up, almost everyone came up to say a few words to her privately. Several of them were already her patients.

Abby tried not to appear as if her attention was divided, but it was. She was watching to see if Kyle would merely leave with Marcie without stopping to say something. Anything.

She wanted to thank him for the flowers.

She wanted him to allude to their getting together again.

She was, Abby realized abruptly, suffering from the morning-after syndrome, despite the fact that there had been more than a few days since their night of love-making.

Were the flowers a consolation prize? A nice way to achieve closure? Or the beginning of something more?

At the moment, she felt thirty-two, going on sixteen.

She was really too old to have her heart leap up just because a good-looking man she happened to have slept with was approaching her. But lectures did no good when they were applied to herself.

Everyone else, she noticed, had left or was leaving. Katie was taking a little longer than she should to gather her notes together, no doubt hoping to see what would happen. The look Abby sent her did nothing to usher her friend on her way.

"Well, you two certainly looked as if you knew what you were doing," Abby commented when Marcie and Kyle reached her. She slipped an arm around Marcie. "Have these classes made you feel any better?"

Marcie shrugged. Turning, she pushed the pillow into

Kyle's arms. He was already holding the comforter she'd been using. "I don't know. The closer it gets, the more nervous I am."

Abby nodded. She'd heard that before, time and again. "Perfectly natural."

Her cheeks looked flushed, Kyle noted. He found himself wanting to rub his thumb over each one, to trace the outline of her lips with his fingers before he satisfied his need to taste them. Banking down the thoughts, he looked at his sister instead.

"What isn't natural is having to do this without a husband." The old complaint rose effortlessly to his tongue. Marcie's state still bothered him. Though it was hard, he'd made it a point to get to know Billy, and the kid really had a lot of promise. And most of all, he loved Marcie. It was Marcie who was stubbornly resisting. Life was tough enough on a woman, without her having people looking down their noses at her for having a baby out of wedlock.

Marcie checked her watch and made a small hissing noise between her teeth. Her glance at Kyle held barely veiled accusation. "You haven't mentioned that for almost two hours. I guess that makes it some kind of record."

Abby placed herself between them physically, the way she wanted to emotionally. "I thought you two decided to table this discussion for a while." Out of the corner of her eye, she saw Katie retreating. That left the three of them together in the large room.

Marcie gave a sharp nod in Kyle's direction. "I did, he didn't."

This could escalate really fast. Marcie's due date was soon, and Abby didn't want anything to upset the girl. She slipped her arm around Marcie's shoulders again.

"Okay, what do you say we stop by the coffee shop down the street for something to drink and a few words?"

Bewildered, Marcie stared at her doctor. "Drink? But I can't—"

"I was thinking along the lines of hot chocolate. With whipped cream on top."

Marcie's eyes gleamed. "Oh."

Kyle had been thinking along the lines of something smooth and on the rocks to help him temporarily manage both his blanketed anger and his blanketed desire. Hot chocolate didn't have a prayer. "Oh."

Abby caught the disappointment in his voice. Caught a great deal more in his eyes. Her stomach flipped over and played dead—for approximately three seconds. She laughed, slipping her arm through his. It didn't feel too bad being in the middle, at least not this time.

"I'm sure they can come up with something stronger for you," she promised.

THE COFFEE SHOP was a short block from the clinic. Abby chose it because of its subdued atmosphere. She was hoping it would encourage Marcie and Kyle to keep their conversation low-key, as well. At Austin Eats, the diner next to the clinic, which she usually frequented after hours, the boisterous, noisy ambience would probably egg them on to a shouting match.

As they walked into the cosy interior, the aroma of exotic coffees blended with the rich scent of wood rose up to greet them.

"This place is a termite's idea of heaven," Abby quipped, sitting down at the nearest empty table for three.

Kyle pushed in his sister's chair and took his own

seat. He would have ushered in Abby's, as well, but she was too quick for him.

"Are you always this self-sufficient?" he asked. Raising a hand, he signaled to a green-aproned waitress.

"Whenever possible." Abby paused as the waitress took their orders, then waited until they were alone again. She knew that Kyle wouldn't want this next part broadcast. "I want you to know I've decided to break my rule and side with Marcie."

It was hard to say who looked more surprised, Marcie or Kyle. But the latter was more vocal.

Kyle had wanted her to support him, but he'd resigned himself to her neutrality. Though he'd all but given up trying to get Marcie to see things his way, this new alliance had the hairs rising at the back of his neck.

"What?"

This wasn't easy for Abby, especially in light of her growing feelings for him. But matters of conscience weren't meant to be easy, just obeyed. She tried to get him to understand. "Marriage is a hard enough thing to make work without added pressures."

The waitress returned, bestowing plain coffee on Kyle, a latte on Abby and a hot chocolate mocha almond on Marcie.

Kyle could barely keep his words back until she retreated. "What pressure? I'll be paying for everything. Hell, I wish someone had come along and paid for everything for me when I was Marcie's age."

Abby laid a hand on Marcie's, stopping the words that she knew were rising to her lips. She knew she could answer Kyle less heatedly. "No," she said firmly. "You don't."

His temper frayed a little further. "So now you can read my mind?"

Abby stood her ground, refusing to be intimidated by the look in his eyes. A look that warned her to back off. "No, but I know your type. You're proud and independent. You would have hated having everything handed to you. You needed to go out and earn it. That's what made it all yours—earning it."

She had him pegged, but he didn't have to like it. He waved a hand at her assessment. "What does that have to do with Marcie and Billy?"

"Billy, I don't know," Abby said honestly. "But Marcie's like you. Stubborn and proud, and she wants to be able to make her own decisions in her own time." She didn't have to look at the girl's face to know that she had described her innermost feelings to a tee.

Kyle's eyes narrowed. "Like getting pregnant?"

Abby heard Marcie's sharp intake of breath and knew the girl was on the verge of exploding and telling Kyle exactly what she thought. And where he could put his benevolent generosity. Abby held up a hand like a traffic cop halting the flow of cars.

"That wasn't a decision—that was something that happened. The decision was to keep the baby, both before birth and after. Don't you think if Marcie had thought it would work out between them from the start, she'd have said yes immediately?"

"Then why did she make love with him?" Kyle demanded.

Marcie's small fist came down in the middle of the table, sending cups trembling atop their saucers. Both sets of eyes turned in her direction. "Hey, 'she' is here. Talk to me."

Kyle blew out a long breath, swallowing an oath that had no business surfacing here. "Talking to you doesn't seem to be doing any good, does it?"

Anger creased Marcie's features and her eyes clouded over with tears. Without a word, she rose and left the table, moving as quickly as her size permitted her to go.

For a second, Abby could only stare at Marcie's retreating back. How had this blown up so fast? She looked at Kyle, tried to curb her accusatory tone. "Well, that went well."

"Maybe you'd better bow out for now." He bit off the words and threw several bills on the table.

Stunned, Abby felt her mouth drop open before she recovered and closed it again. "You were the one who dragged me into the middle of this," she pointed out.

But she doubted that Kyle even heard her. He was hurrying out the door after his sister.

JANELLE FLEW across the length of the hotel room at the sound of the first knock, and yanked open the door. She'd nearly gone out of her mind, waiting. He was two hours late.

"What the hell kept you?"

It wasn't the sort of greeting Petey had been hoping for. But then, he never quite knew what to expect when it came to Janelle. She blew hot and cold at the same time. He didn't much care for the cold. She was cynical and calculating when she was cold. But when she blew hot…it was all worth it.

He was too tired to put up with her abuse now. "Damn plane ran into turbulance. We couldn't land. Hell, woman, if you're going to glare at me like that, I'll just turn around and go back home."

Janelle bridled her anger and caught Petey's arm before he could turn away. She thought fast on her feet. It was her best asset.

"No, baby, don't go. I'm sorry. It's just that I missed you so." Pressing her body to his, she kissed him with just enough passion to make him manageable. When he reached for her, she danced back on the balls of her feet, just out of reach. "Uh-uh. First I get to see the artwork." Her eyes narrowed. "You did get it, didn't you?"

"Yeah, I got it." He didn't like lying to her, but he liked her temper even less.

"Well, let's see it, let's see it." Not waiting for him to comply, she quickly yanked the ends of his blue denim shirt out of his jeans and raised the material to his chest. Excitement telegraphed itself through Janelle, filling her veins, making her head spin.

He'd gotten it, just as she'd told him to.

It was all coming together. Her plan was finally coming together.

The edgy thrill brought impatience in its wake. She wanted this to be over, wanted to finally take what was hers. She didn't want to wait anymore.

But she had to.

Holding the edges of the shirt in her hands, she dug her slick, red-tipped fingernails into her palms, willing herself to calm down.

When this was over, she was going to lie naked on a bed of hundred-dollar bills—no, thousand-dollar bills—and just roll over them, absorbing the scent of the money through her pores.

Her smile widened at the thought.

Yanking the sides of her husband's shirt apart, she stripped it off his shoulders and looked hard at the tattoo.

"Perfect." She all but purred the word. For once, he'd done something right. Pacified, she could afford to be kind. Petey performed better when she was kind to him. "And see, baby? It didn't hurt a bit, did it?"

"Hurt enough," he mumbled.

Petey knew his limitations, knew he wasn't as smart as the woman he'd married. But he also knew Janelle. If he agreed too readily, she would smell a rat and maybe find out that it wasn't a real crescent-shaped tattoo on his belly, but some very fancy artwork, courtesy of his sister. He didn't need to hear Janelle bitching about it.

Janelle ran the tip of her tongue along her lips, knowing what the sensual movement did to Petey. Her voice dropped an octave as her eyes slowly roamed over him. She realized that the sight of the tattoo was turning her on.

Or maybe it was the promise of the money it would bring.

"When you're rolling in money, you won't remember a thing about that old needle. As for now, let me make it up to you, sugar."

She unhooked the single catch at her waist, and the red dress suddenly hung loose on her frame. She tugged it off and stood before her husband in little more than black lacy scraps that on a less-endowed woman might have served as adequate cover. On Janelle, they hardly hid the essentials.

She saw the lust enter Petey's eyes. It empowered her. She could always count on him to think with that part of his body first.

Easier than leading a man around by his nose, she thought. The throaty laugh echoed in the room, melding with the sound of Petey's heavy breathing.

Slowly moving against him, her eyes on his, she slipped her hand down into his jeans. "Ooh, you are happy to see me, baby, aren't you? See, you do as I ask you to, and I'll make nice. You won't regret listening to me. Ever.'' She breathed the word against his face, her lips a scant quarter-inch away from his.

She knew how to tantalize him, knew how to make him do exactly what she wanted.

She was counting on it.

CHAPTER FOURTEEN

EXHAUSTION HAD HOLLOWED OUT her insides and taken with it most of her tolerance.

Feeling uncustomarily short-tempered and irritable, Abby dropped down into the first chair she came to after arriving home. Her purse was on the floor, listing to one side beside the shoes she'd stepped out of the second she'd set foot inside the door.

Drained, she was sorely tempted to remain exactly where she was, without moving a muscle, until morning intruded again.

It wasn't so much that it had been a hectic day. For once, there had been no emergency deliveries, no appointments to squeeze in between neatly scheduled ones. Even the press had deigned to back off a bit in their all-consuming quest to information about the 'mystery baby' now residing in her mother's house. Although on that front, she mused, they had found a sidebar to sink their fangs into.

For reasons completely unfathomable to her, the press thought that there was reader mileage in the allegations that Ellie had won her position as Maitland Maternity's chief administrator solely through nepotism instead of incredibly hard work.

Denial was useless, so the family was waiting for this, too, to run out of steam. It seemed that the Maitlands were forever waiting for one furor or another to die down. At times, it was emotionally wearing.

As wearing as some people.

Abby sighed deeply and frowned. She felt as if she were in the lead car of a long roller coaster, plummeting down a very steep incline whose end was nowhere in sight.

That meant there was no end to the sinking feeling, either.

Served her right for getting entangled with the likes of Kyle McDermott and his thousand-watt smile instead of sticking to what she knew best: her work. She decided that men were not only the opposite sex in every sense of the word, they were a completely alien species—warm one minute, distant the next. And utterly, utterly un-understandable. She certainly hadn't been able to break the code.

Nor was she going to try any longer.

She hadn't heard a word from Kyle since last night, when he'd gone out after Marcie. He'd left Abby to deal with her frustration, not to mention walk back to the clinic's parking lot for her car.

Idiot.

She had no idea if she was reserving the term for Kyle for being Kyle, or for herself for caring.

What she needed more than to sit here like a warmed-over lump of clay, Abby decided, was a hot bubble bath. One that would last for as long as it took to leach Kyle McDermott and his intoxicating hold on her out of her system. She wondered if there was a chance of heating up the Hoover Dam and just soaking in it for the rest of eternity.

To turn the bubble bath into the cleansing ritual she so desperately needed, Abby put on a CD of gentle rain forest sounds and wearily slipped her tense body into the whipped mound of seductive suds.

The doorbell chimed.

"Why me?" she murmured impatiently.

Sinking down farther into the tub so that the suds were up to her neck, Abby debated ignoring the irritating intrusion. Probably just someone selling magazines. Eventually, they would tire of leaning on the bell and go away.

But they didn't. The doorbell chimed repeatedly, jarring the mood she was desperately seeking to create.

Muttering under her breath, Abby dragged herself out of the water. Suds clung to her body as she threw on an ankle-length white terry-cloth robe and tied it at her waist. She was still muttering as she made her way down the stairs.

And the doorbell was still ringing.

Maybe it was important. Doubt and concern wedged beneath her weary anger. Her family didn't usually call ahead before stopping by.

"Who is it?" she called out, hurrying the rest of the way to the door.

"Flower delivery," a high-pitched voice informed her. Flowers? Abby unlocked the door and pulled it open. And found herself looking up at Kyle's face.

The rest of his torso was blocked by what appeared to be more than two dozen long-stemmed yellow roses that broke over the mouth of the vase in wild profusion.

He'd been right, Kyle thought, to use the phony voice to lull her into opening the door. The look in her eyes the second after she saw him registered barely suppressed annoyance.

Not that he didn't deserve it.

He summoned his most compelling expression and

hoped he could muddle his way through this. It was new territory he was traversing. But then, it seemed that all the territory he was crossing since Abby had entered his life was new and uncharted.

Abby stared at the roses, then at Kyle. Instead of his usual three-piece suit, he was wearing a work shirt, jeans and boots. He looked like a cowboy who'd come courting. She was acutely conscious of the fact that she wasn't wearing anything beneath her robe. Her pulse began to scramble, and she called herself a fool.

She did her best to seem uninterested as she nodded toward the flowers. "Starting your own route?"

He looked past her shoulder. "Can I come in?"

Abby stood her ground. He'd already trespassed enough in her life. "Why? I can sign for the flowers right here."

He knew she was angry, and he figured she had a right to be. In her place, he would be, too. But he was miserable, too. More miserable than he'd thought possible, and at a loss as to how to make amends. So he thrust the flowers into her hands, driving her back as he did so.

Once inside, he shut the door behind him. He wished there was a way to stall longer. Or for her to forgive his behavior without his actually coming out and asking her to do so.

"I went back to the coffee shop, you know, but you'd already left." Uncomfortable, he shoved his hands into his pockets and turned to look at her. "Look, saying I'm sorry doesn't come easy to me."

Abby wasn't about to make it any easier for him, either. She wasn't completely sure if she believed him about returning to the coffee shop. Even if he had, he hadn't called her last night, hadn't attempted to explain the fact that he'd stormed off in anger.

Abby raised her chin. "No, but apparently hurting people's feelings does."

The coldness in her voice hit him with the force of an iceberg. He'd expected her to be angry, but not hurt. This put a much worse spin on things.

"Granted, I had no right to say what I did. To behave the way I did. I shouldn't have walked out on you. But I did come back." He felt himself stumbling. "Marcie was running off, and I was angry—"

She laughed shortly. "No kidding."

For a second, she felt like throwing the flowers aside, vase and all, and venting her own anger. But that would only make a mess she'd have to clean up later. And besides, there was no reason to take things out on the flowers.

"But if I didn't care—" Kyle stopped abruptly.

He dragged a hand impatiently through his hair, realizing that he was admitting more than he had intended to. He was still wrestling with, still exploring, these newfound feelings himself. Letting Abby in on them before he knew what he was dealing with wasn't part of his plan.

"Hell, this is not coming out right." He all but glared at her for putting him through this. "Just say you accept my apology, and we'll call it even."

"What apology?" Turning her back on him, she set the vase on the table.

Kyle turned her around again to face him. "My apology."

Abby's eyes narrowed. Talk about a halfhearted attempt. "You didn't apologize about anything. You said apologies didn't come easy, that's all. In order to accept something, I have to be made aware of it.''

Kyle swallowed the curse that rose to his lips, and laughed dryly, instead. "You're not going to make this easy, are you?''

Abby shook her head slowly, her eyes never leaving his. "Nope.''

Kyle searched her eyes for a hint of humor to let him know where he stood. He remained in the dark. "I guess I have that coming.''

He reminded himself how he'd felt when, after securing Marcie in the car with a promise to stay put, he'd returned to the coffee shop to find Abby gone. Empty, hollow. And damn confused. Remembering that, he let it guide his words.

He took her hands in his. "I'm sorry. I didn't mean to walk out on you like that, didn't mean to blame you for the fact that I couldn't—'' Words were turning to raw cotton in his mouth. "Are you wearing anything under that robe?''

"What I have or don't have under this robe has nothing to do with anything. You were doing very well with your apology—for a novice. Continue.''

"I can't,'' he told her honestly. He couldn't stop staring at her robe. The two halves were beginning to work their way apart with every movement she made, sending his thoughts to places that had nothing to do with apologies. "I keep wanting to peel that off you and find out if I'm right.''

She took a step back. He got the message. Business first, then pleasure. "I am sorry, Abby. Very, very sorry.'' In a swift movement, he hooked two fingers under her belt and pulled her to him. His grin was wide and sexy, and it seduced her with a speed that took her breath away. "You're not, are you?"

"Sorry?" she guessed, cocking her head.

She knew damn well what he meant. "No, wearing anything under that."

Abby shook her head slowly, humor glinting in her eyes. Instead of answering his question, she pretended to mourn the aborted attempt at an apology. "And you were doing so well, too."

"I can do better." His arms enfolded her, and he touched his lips to the side of her neck. The leap of her pulse rewarded him. He was forgiven, he thought. Relief washed over him. "Let me show you how really sorry I am."

She could feel her knees turning to water already. It didn't take long, Abby thought. "Sorry is the last word that comes to mind when you do that."

"Good."

His mouth covered hers and miraculously replaced exhaustion with exhilaration. Her blood quickened so fast that it made her senses spin almost out of control.

She felt him slip first one hand beneath her robe, and then the other. Her body tingled instantly, reacting to his touch, his warmth. Her breath caught as arrows of desire were released, flying off in all directions.

Like a woman reborn, she began to tug on his clothes, to separate buttons from their holes, while his hands caressed, molded, teased. Primed her until her every thought, her every movement focused on making love with him. As she divested him of his shirt and then his jeans, Abby was aware of her robe slipping slowly from her shoulders, coaxed by his hands. Instantly she felt the heat of his body, the warmth of his passion as he pressed her to him, lowering her to the rug.

Kyle was stunned at how much he wanted her. Wanted her sweetness, her innocence. Wanted her wide-eyed pleasure in what they shared.

It was startling to realize that she was both independent and dependent, strong and vulnerable. Sophisticated and childlike. She was many things to him. And the awe and satisfaction at being with her was overwhelming.

Desire overtook him, both of the flesh and the mind.

He wanted to give her pleasure, endless pleasure, not just to satisfy her, but to wipe away the memory of whoever it was that had hurt her, whoever it was that had left that soiled imprint on her soul that made her so cautious, so wary.

He wanted her, Kyle realized with a sudden jolt, to love him.

His breath backed up in his lungs as he pulled his head back and look at her.

Dazed, Abby blinked, trying to focus her eyes. Her mind. There was a look on his face she couldn't place. "What?"

The smile was slow, working its way into her blood. "I just had a revelation."

"What?" she breathed again. Afraid, hopeful. She could feel her heart pounding in her head.

But he couldn't tell her, not in so many words—not yet. It wouldn't be fair to either of them. He wasn't sure himself whether this was the moment making him feel this way, or something more. Things said in haste carried the penalty—and the pain—of forever.

So instead, he pressed his lips to her throat and whispered, "That I want to make love to you for a very long, long time."

The admission sent her heart scurrying every which

way. Were these just empty words said in the heat of the moment? Or did he really mean them?

No, she wasn't going to wrestle with doubts. If he was just talking, she'd deal with it later. Now she wanted to have him hold her, to make love with her, to make her forget every negative thought she'd ever had. She needed to forget. To just enjoy him and this wonderful feeling he created inside her.

She curved her body into his, giving herself freely. Asking for nothing in return. Kyle felt humbled. It made him want to give her everything. It made him begin to think of forever.

Forever.

The word stood before him, seventy feet tall, scaring the hell out of him. He banked down his fear, determined to concentrate only on the here and now.

And the woman in his arms.

Abby pressed her lips together to keep from whimpering. From begging for more. His mouth was roaming her body, setting small fires in its wake that grew until they all but consumed her. She dug her fingertips into the rug beneath her, twisting and turning. Unable to deal with this much ecstasy, unwilling to relinquish it.

She could no longer sustain a coherent thought, for she was elevated to a state of pure lights and magic, passions and needs. And desperately, desperately wanting to remain in this safe haven where there were physical pleasures the likes of which were far beyond her wildest dreams.

Abby caught her bottom lip between her teeth as she felt Kyle's tongue trailing along her belly, dipping lower. Sending a series of explosions shooting through her limbs. Arching her hips, she cried out as her body was raised to one shimmering peak and then another.

Barely able to see, Abby reached for him. Her fingers caught air before making contact with his shoulders.

"If you don't take me now, there's not going to be anything left to take." It was half entreaty, half threat.

Kyle grinned. Very slowly, aware of the effect it had on both of them, he drew his body over hers. The sheen of perspiration that greeted him sent another salvo of excitement through him.

"Can't have that," he breathed heavily against her ear.

Framing her face with his hands, Kyle gently brushed back the hair from her forehead. She seemed to glow from within, making her more beautiful to him than ever.

My God, he was in love with her. The thought thundered across his brain. He fought to drive it away.

Unable to hold himself in check any longer, he slipped into her, his pulse quickening as he felt her tighten around him. With slow, deliberate movements, he began to stroke her. And himself.

She could feel his heart beating against hers. Pounding against hers. It increased the frenzy she was already feeling.

As the fever pitch grew, she almost cried out what she knew she had to hold back. Almost told him that she loved him. The realization filled her with wonder. With joy.

And fear.

She'd been here before and had garnered only ashes. But this was Kyle...

Her arms tightened around him as the last explosion shook her. She felt him shudder against her and knew that she hadn't experienced it alone.

Determined to hang on to it, to him and the feelings

they'd created between them, Abby squeezed her eyes shut, her arms entwined around him. She held on for dear life. For this, to her, *was* life.

Opening his eyes, Kyle drew his head back and looked down at her. A sense of wonder filled him. He was hardly a novice at this, and yet he felt like one. Felt, too, that what he had somehow blindly stumbled onto was very, very precious.

"It just keeps getting better, doesn't it?" he whispered to her. He saw that she was biting her lower lip, struggling with something. "What?" He didn't realize he was holding his breath as he asked.

"I don't know whether to be coy or to be myself." Even her asking seemed to stack the weight on one side, she thought.

"Yourself, Abby, just be yourself."

But she still had doubts. Doubts about him, about what she was feeling for him. If she trusted him with her heart and he broke it, what would she have then? It couldn't be rebuilt a second time. She was certain of that. "What if that isn't good enough?"

"It's good enough," he whispered against her temple. Kyle moved his head back until his eyes held hers. "For me."

She felt as if her heart had slammed into her chest. Damn him if he was lying to her. And damn her for believing. But she couldn't help herself. "Then yes, it does keep getting better." She tried to hedge her bets, instinctively knowing it was already too late to protect her heart. "Do you think that's because this is still new between us?"

"Honestly?"

Her heart suddenly hovered between beats, waiting. "Honestly."

Kyle smiled into her eyes. "No."

Then, thinking perhaps he had said too much, he rolled off. He wasn't accustomed to placing almost all his cards on the table. Wasn't accustomed to feeling this uncertain about his fate. Not anymore.

But the loss of intimate contact immediately left him feeling as if something dear had been lost. He gathered her to him and breathed in the scent that clung to her skin. And to his.

He pressed a kiss to her hair. "I think it's just going to keep getting better for a long, long time." Something stirred within him. "You know, it's only been such a short time, but I'm not sure now how I managed to face every day without you in it before."

Fear wouldn't let her savor his words. Men didn't fall in love in a heartbeat. Only women did. "Don't say things you don't mean."

Sensing she was about to get up, he tightened his arms around her, holding her in place. Maybe he was going too fast. Too fast for both of them. He tried to make light of it. "I never lie to beautiful women, especially when they're lying nude next to me."

He was teasing her, and yet there was something in his eyes. Something that told her he was hiding behind the banter. Not to lie, but to protect. Was he as afraid of this as she was? It didn't seem possible.

And yet...

A smile creased her lips as she looked at him. "That would put you in a class by yourself."

He felt something stir within him, something that was taking hold so quickly that he didn't know which way to turn. And he found himself meeting it instead of moving away. "I may not be in a class by myself, but I'm not *him,* either."

She stiffened slightly. "Him?"

He ran his hand along her arm, stroking it. Soothing her. "The guy you told me about. I don't need your money, Abby, or your prestige."

Her eyes met his. "What do you need?"

"Just you."

Abby moistened her lips, but her throat remained dry. "I'd like to believe you."

"But?"

A faint smile lifted the corners of her mouth. He could read her pretty well. "But I hate being a fool, Kyle."

His fingertips grazed her face. "And making love with me makes you a fool?"

She couldn't think straight anymore. Later, she'd sort this out. Now, all she wanted to do was feel.

"Not making love with you would make me a fool," she quipped. Sliding back onto the floor, she linked her arms behind his neck. "I don't want to talk anymore."

Just as he brought his mouth to hers, the telephone on the coffee table just above her head rang.

CHAPTER FIFTEEN

KYLE DREW AWAY, and glanced up at the ringing phone. "Do you want to answer that?"

He was being understanding. Resigned, she nodded. The last thing she wanted right now was to have to rush off somewhere. Praying it was a wrong number, Abby felt around for the telephone just above her. Securing the receiver, she brought to her ear.

"Hello, this is Abby Maitland."

"Help me."

The plea, almost too weak to hear, had Abby bolting upright. "Who is this?"

Kyle saw every muscle in her body tense. Concerned, he scrambled up beside her. "What is it?"

Abby shook her head, turning from him. She couldn't afford to be distracted now. Someone needed her. She covered her other ear with her hand, trying to make out the faint voice on the other end of the line. Was that whimpering?

"Speak up, I can't hear you."

The person on the other end of the line struggled to be coherent. "Abby...please come. It's...Marcie... I..."

Fear galvanized her. On her feet in an instant, she hurried into her bedroom. Her clothes were scattered all over the bed where she had thrown them. She snatched up her underwear and started to dress, the phone lodged between her shoulder and ear. All the while, she tried to keep her voice calm.

"Where are you calling from, honey?" Marcie was a strong, healthy girl. There was every indication that hers would be a normal, unremarkable delivery. What had gone wrong?

"Home." It was more of a sob than a word. Abby had the impression that Kyle's sister was fighting for consciousness. "Blood... There's blood... Oh, God, Abby." Her voice rose. "I'm so scared."

Shifting the portable receiver from one hand to the other, Abby yanked on her pullover, then grabbed her skirt. She saw Kyle, his jeans already on, looking at her from her doorway.

"I'll be right there. Hang up the phone. Kyle will call you back on the cell phone. You can talk to him while we're on our way." She saw the worried look in Kyle's eyes.

"I—I—" Marcie sounded as if she was gasping. Abby tried not to let her own mind go into overdrive. "I—I—"

"Hang up the phone, Marcie," she enunciated. "He'll call you. I promise."

Kyle was instantly at her side, nearly tripping over her robe.

"Marcie? It's Marcie?" He grabbed for the receiver, but Abby had already disconnected. She tossed the phone on her bed as she hurried from the room. Her shoes, she remembered, were still by the front door.

"Get your cell phone—call her on that. We've got to get over to your place."

"What happened?" He jammed his bare feet into his boots, and shoved his socks into his pocket. The cell phone was on the floor where his shirt had been.

"I don't know." Having stopped only to get the medical bag she kept in the hall closet and to scoop up her purse from the floor, Abby was already out the door. "She's not due for another two weeks, but if there's anything I've learned, it's that nothing is written in stone when it comes to having babies."

THEY TOOK ABBY'S CAR. She slid behind the wheel and Kyle followed, getting in on the passenger side. They were already in the street as he flipped open his phone. "I'll call 9-1-1."

"No, call her," Abby urged. "We'll get there before they do."

This wasn't the first race with the stork she'd been involved in, and she knew the ins and outs. Kyle's house was only twelve minutes away. Ten, if she caught all the lights. Abby tried to give him an encouraging smile. For now, she saw no point in saying anything about the blood Marcie had mentioned. He'd see it soon enough.

"She might just be panicking." It was an effort to sound calm. The terror in Marcie's voice came back to her. "Contractions can be a pretty frightening thing when you're eighteen and all by yourself."

"I knew I should have hired a live-in housekeeper." His privacy should have taken a back seat to his sister's needs. Something else he was going to have to re-evaluate, Kyle thought in exasperation. He hit the key that would automatically connect him to his home number. The busy signal did nothing to calm his mounting agitation. "It's busy."

"Maybe she's calling back to say it's a false alarm." But Abby didn't think so. She flew through a yellow light just as it turned red. Habit had her glancing into the rearview mirror, but there were no dancing red-and-blue lights in her wake. One traffic light down, half a dozen to go.

Kyle nodded, trying to convince himself that Abby was right. Marcie was probably just overreacting. Levelheaded though she had always seemed, since becoming pregnant, his sister had turned into a veritable basket of emotions. There had been enough highs and lows in the last eight-and-a-half months to please the most ardent roller-coaster enthusiast. That was it, he told himself. Due soon, Marcie was undoubtedly panicking.

He hung on to that thought as the busy signal buzzed in his ear.

Annoyed, he slapped the cover back on the cell phone, breaking the connection. Abby whizzed through another intersection just as the lights turned. The sharp left she made had him sliding toward her.

Kyle grabbed the dashboard as she took another corner. "Where did you learn to drive like that?"

Despite the situation, she grinned. Maybe it was nerves. "College. I was always oversleeping." She swallowed a curse as she had to come to a full stop. Running a light wasn't in her repertoire. She took the moment to place her hand over his. "Don't worry, it's going to be okay."

It had to be. Kyle stared straight head, willing them there already. "Yeah."

THE CAR HAD NOT YET COME to a full stop in his driveway, when Kyle threw open the passenger door and leaped out. By the time Abby yanked up the hand brake, he was jamming the key into the front door.

He left it hanging open, and ran in ahead of her. "Marcie! Marcie, where are you?"

He was bellowing loud enough for his voice to carry throughout the house, but he heard no answer.

This is bad, he thought, and called out again. "Marcie!"

A heartbeat behind him, the medical bag that R.J. had bestowed on her at graduation in her hands, Abby quickly looked around. There was no indication that the girl was home, but they had made it in nine minutes flat. Marcie *had* to be here.

"Check upstairs, I'll check down here."

The instruction was needless. Kyle was already taking the stairs, two at a time.

"Marcie, damn it, answer me!" Fear had roughened his voice, making it stern. "Where the hell are you?"

There was no time to appreciate the sleek layout of the custom-built house, or to take in any of its sophisticated decorating scheme. It was all a colorful blur as Abby hurried from one room to another, calling Marcie's name. Fear began to grip her.

"Oh, God."

Abby's heart stopped a second after she crossed the kitchen threshold. Marcie's legs projected beyond the work counter. Hurrying around the island, she found the girl sprawled across the floor, the receiver still clutched in her hands. Her eyes were open, but she seemed disoriented and dazed.

"Kyle, I found her! She's in the kitchen!" Abby called out, dropping to her knees.

She made a quick assessment. Marcie was pale, but there were no pools of blood on the floor the way she'd been envisioning. Abby took the girl's hands into hers, set aside the receiver.

"Marcie, it's Abby. Can you focus?" She held her

hand up in front of the girl's face. "How many fingers do you see?"

Gulping in air, Marcie began to cry.

"It's okay, Marcie, it's going to be okay." Afraid to let her personal involvement cloud her judgment, Abby tried again. "How many fingers, Marcie? How many do you see?"

"All of them," she sobbed. "Three." She clutched wildly at Abby's hand as the pain began again. "Oh, Abby, the room was spinning. And everything started going black. I think I hit my head when I fell." The contraction intensified, and she cried out, squeezing harder. "The baby, what's going to happen to the baby?" Terror filled her young eyes. "Abby—"

"Sh, it's all right," Abby said soothingly. She leaned over for a better look at Marcie's wound. "Let me see what you did to your head."

A single touch showed her that the dark hair was sticky and slightly matted. Marcie had sustained a good-size gash, but nothing life-threatening. Rocking back on her heels, Abby saw that the corner of Marcie's dress was damp. Closer examination confirmed what Abby feared. The fall had caused Marcie's water to break. Marcie was in labor.

Abby felt the girl's fingers digging into her urgently. "The baby, it's coming, Abby. I feel it." She started to panic. "I didn't hurt it, did I? It's going to be all right, isn't it? The baby—"

Abby mentally crossed her fingers. "Everything's going to be fine."

She didn't hear Kyle come in, but the next moment, he was beside her, stunned and shaken and obviously grappling with fear. An oath on his lips, he began to elbow her aside, slipping his powerful hands under his sister. Marcie whimpered as he tried to pick her up.

Abby caught his arm quickly, stopping him. "Don't move her just yet."

"But she can't stay on the floor."

God, she hoped he wasn't going to get in the way. "Call the clinic. Have them send the ambulance out. Your niece or nephew's about to make his or her debut. Marcie cut her head going down, but I don't know if there's any other damage. I don't want to risk moving her."

A queasiness overtook Kyle. His first instinct was to back away, to use one of the other telephones located throughout the house. He didn't want to be here, didn't want to see the pain that Marcie was going through.

But the look in his sister's eyes as she turned them toward him erased all thoughts from his mind but one. He had to help her any way he could.

"Okay." Sinking to his knees, he took Marcie's hand in his. As he held the cell phone in his other hand, he pressed out the numbers Abby recited. The call was picked up on the second ring. He gave the address and Abby's assessment, then rang off.

He shoved the phone into his back pocket. "What do you want me to do?" The question was directed at Abby, even though he kept his eyes on Marcie.

Wishing for sterile conditions was out of the question. Abby slipped on a pair of disposable gloves. "Put your coaching skills to work. Your little sister's going to need them."

Panic flared again in Marcie's eyes. She wrapped her fingers even more tightly around her brother's wrist, like a little girl, lost and frightened.

"Kyle, I'm scared, so scared."

"I'm right here, baby." Smoothing back his sister's hair, he looked over in Abby's direction. There was something about her, about the confidence she radiated, that comforted him. "We're both right here. Nothing's going to happen to you, Marcie."

"It's like falling off a log," Abby assured her. Very carefully, she lifted Marcie's skirt and pushed it back. Marcie whimpered, arching on the floor as she bit back a scream. "A very big log," Abby amended. "Yell if you have to, Marcie. It really does help."

"Uh-huh." But the contraction was already receding, loosening its hold on her. Marcie exhaled, though she looked as if she were fearfully anticipating the next one. She gazed up at Kyle beseechingly. "Kyle, all those arguments…I'm sorry."

"No, you're not." Worried, he managed to force a smile to his lips for her sake. When she was a little girl, she'd always taken her cue from him. It placed a great deal of responsibility on his shoulders at the time. But looking back, he knew it had had a great deal to do with forming the man he was now. "Once this is over, you'll pick a dozen more with me. And we'll enjoy them all." He closed his other hand over hers. "The kid'll grow up to be a referee." He could see the tension entering her body. His mind scrambled to recall what he'd learned in class with her. "Now stop saying things you don't mean, and just concentrate on breathing."

Marcie caught her lip between her teeth. "Easy for you to say."

"No," he told her meaningfully, "it's not." And then he grew serious. He wanted this to be over even more than she did. "But for once in your life, you're going to do as I say. Deep breaths, Marcie. Now."

Glancing over, he saw Abby watching him, her

mouth curved in approval. The intimate look, born of a communion of souls rather than bodies, warmed him. Made him feel even closer to her than when they had made love.

It was a hell of a time for a man to come to a momentous decision…on his knees, coaching his sister to bring her child into the world. But, he reasoned, he supposed it was as good a time as any.

The feeling that everything was going to be all right pervaded him, slicing through the steely bands of panic that had so recently threatened to close around him.

Abby couldn't believe how quickly Marcie had dilated. They had arrived none too soon. Taking out a bottle of antiseptic, she gently swabbed the area, then placed the surgical scissors on the clean cloth she'd laid out. She nodded when Kyle raised a brow in her direction. They were almost there.

"First babies are usually slow in coming, but this little tiger is an exception."

"What do you want? He's a McDermott." Kyle looked down at Marcie. Memories crowded his mind. "Right, Marcie?"

"Right." Her breath hitched. Another contraction was coming, Kyle thought. "And…a…Madison."

"So you've decided to marry Billy, after all?" Funny, a few hours ago, that would have meant something to him. Now he no longer cared. All he wanted was for his sister to be happy. And safe.

"Someday," Marcie allowed, trying to conserve her breath. "When…he's…ripe."

"We shall pick no husband before his time." Abby couldn't help paraphrasing the old slogan. The smile was in her eyes as she raised them to look at Marcie.

Kyle braced himself, as his sister began tightening

her fingers around his again. Wishing he could take her pain away, he lightly stroked her arm. "Well, you don't ever have to marry him if you don't want to. You don't have to do anything you don't want to."

Marcie turned her head toward him and managed a smile, albeit a small one.

"Does that mean...I...can get someone else...to have...this baby?"

The time for talking had passed. Abby snapped to attention. "Sorry, too late. Marcie, I see the crown." She looked at Kyle, grateful that despite his protests, he wasn't the type to fall apart at a time like this. "Okay, I want you to prop up her shoulders so she's almost sitting up." She turned her eyes to the girl. "Marcie, I want you to push, but only when I tell you to. And I want you to stop when I say so."

"Stop?" Marcie wanted this over with. "But—"

"Listen to the doctor, Marce," Kyle ordered. "She's been through this more times than we have." Disengaging his hand, he moved behind Marcie and slowly raised her by her shoulders until she was leaning against him.

Her eyes riveted to the tiny section of the baby's head that she could see, Abby ordered, "Okay, now push. Push hard. Atta girl. You're going great—and stop!"

There was no need to tell Marcie to stop. Panting, the young woman seemed to completely deflate as she fell back against Kyle's hands.

Abby offered her a quick flash of a smile, and then it was show time again. "Okay, push. Harder. C'mon, you can do it."

With a sob, Marcie complied, grunting and nearly screaming at the end, her hands fisted so tightly that they were trembling at her sides. This time, she stopped before Abby told her to. When she slumped against Kyle's hands, she was drenched in perspiration.

Abby took a deep breath, willing air into Marcie's lungs. She silently counted off the time. "Again."

Marcie began to cry as she shook her head from side to side. "I can't."

But this time, it was Kyle who took over. He pushed Marcie up into a near-sitting position again, despite her resistance.

"Yes, you can." His voice was stern. There was no room for refusal. "You can do anything you set your mind to—you always have. Now, the sooner you get this over with, the sooner this baby's going to get here. Ready?" Not waiting for her reply, he gave the order. "Push."

Panting, drained, Marcie squeezed her eyes shut and pushed with every fiber of her being. The effort ended in a shriek.

"Almost there, Marcie," Abby declared, the excitement of the birth getting to her the way it always did. "I got a head. I know it's hard on you, I know you're working hard, but we're almost there," she encouraged her. "Just one more time, honey. Just push for me one more time. C'mon, I know you can do it. I need shoulders, give me shoulders, Marcie."

Bearing down, Marcie made one last great effort. "It feels…like…a lineman…"

Abby released the breath she was holding as she eased the baby out completely. Another miracle, fresh and hot. She felt her heart begin to swell within her breast. How many of these tiny beings had she helped bring into the world? Hers were the first hands that held them.

"Lucky she's not wearing her shoulder pads. Hello, angel," she murmured to the baby.

Marcie could hardly rouse herself. Gratitude flooded her as she felt her brother prop her up one more time so she could see her baby. "She? I, uh, had...a...she?"

"Yes." Abby spared one glance in her direction, smiling broadly. "You had a she. Congratulations, you have a beautiful, messy baby girl."

Awestruck, Kyle lowered Marcie down again, still watching Abby. Abby's hands moved quickly. Using what looked to him like an eyedropper, she cleared the baby's passageways, drawing the fluid from her nose and mouth. A lusty wail followed.

Abby looked up at Kyle. "Got a clean towel? I need a clean towel." As he hurried off to bring her one, she called after him. "Make it two."

He was back faster than she thought possible, handing her two large bath towels. Abby cut the cord, then laughed as she cleaned off the baby. "We could lose her in either one of these." With skilled hands, she wrapped the infant in the second towel. "There, nice and fresh and ready to greet the world." Rising to her feet with the baby in her arms, she looked at Kyle. There was a strange expression on his face. The kind men wore, Abby thought, just before they became putty in a tiny baby's hand. "Would you like to hold her?" she asked him.

He looked hesitant, as if he were afraid the baby would break if he touched her. With the baby cradled against her, Abby arranged his arms. "She's not going to shatter. They're a lot more resilient than you think," she promised.

He felt as if he was on the threshold of a miracle. Emotions he couldn't begin to identify crowded inside him. He fell in love at first sight for the second time in his life.

Except that this time, he thought, glancing at Abby, he knew it immediately instead of having it on delayed relay.

Squatting down, he presented his sister with her daughter. ''Hey, here's your mommy. Be nice to her— she did all the work.'' He saw tears shimmering in Marcie's eyes as she took the baby into her arms.

The doorbell rang.

Abby ran her hand through her hair and blew out a breath. ''Company's always dropping by when you're not ready for them,'' she quipped, then held up a hand as Kyle started to rise. ''No, that's okay. I'll get it. You stay here with Marcie and your niece, and bond.''

Feeling incredibly lighthearted and satisfied with herself, Abby went to answer the door to the clinic's paramedics, a gurney between them.

She recognized both of them. Inez and Bob were already with Maitland Maternity when she formally joined the staff. ''Took you two long enough.'' She held the door open as they came in. ''She's in the kitchen.'' Leading the way, Abby looked over her shoulder at them. ''I did all your work for you.''

''Knew we could count on you, Doc,'' Bob said, flashing a wide, toothy grin. ''How's she doing?''

Abby rattled off the particulars before going over to Marcie. Gently, she eased the baby from her. ''Marcie, this is Inez and Bob. They're going to help me take you to the hospital now.'' She saw the way the girl's eyes darted toward Kyle. ''Don't worry, he'll be right behind you in the car.''

Kyle squeezed Marcie's hand as the two attendants snapped the legs of the gurney into an upright position.

They began wheeling her out of the room. "Couldn't lose me if you tried, Marce," he promised his sister.

"I wouldn't want to," Marcie whispered.

Well, at least that part had ended well, Abby thought, walking in front of them. She glanced down at the baby in her arms and felt the wistfulness setting in again.

She blocked it, the way she had all the other times. Her someday wasn't here yet.

KYLE STOOD IN THE HALL outside the waiting room, unable to sit in the comfortable chairs that had been provided for expectant family members. Impatience slashed at him with an unfamiliar savagery.

What the hell was taking so long?

He'd entered the hospital just in time to see Abby disappearing down the hall with Marcie and the paramedics. None of the nurses would tell him if his sister had been assigned a room yet, or where she was. To take his mind off his concern, he placed a call to Billy to tell him that he was a father.

The phone on the other end rang five times before Kyle heard a male voice say hello. He hesitated before asking, "Billy?"

"Yeah, this is Billy. Who's this?"

Was it him, or did the boy's voice sound younger than he remembered? "Billy, it's Kyle. McDermott. Marcie's brother," he added for good measure when he heard no response.

"I know who you are, Mr. McDermott. Why are you calling me?" And then it suddenly seemed to sink in. "Is it about Marcie? Did something happen to Marcie?"

Kyle was heartened at the sound of concern he heard

in Billy's voice. It seemed genuine enough. "In a manner of speaking. And to you, too."

There was a pause. "I'm not following you."

Well, Marcie had never claimed that Billy was the brightest bulb in the box—just the most loving. And look where that loving had gotten them. "I'm trying to tell you that Marcie had her baby."

"Wow, no kidding?" His voice held wonder coupled with excitement. "What was it?"

It. As if Marcie had gone to FAO Schwartz and picked out a doll. Kyle shook his head as he shifted the pay phone receiver to his other ear. Maybe his sister had been right about Billy, after all. "You have a daughter."

"A daughter? No way. You sure?"

"Very sure. They have ways of telling these things at the hospital."

"Huh?"

Definitely not the brightest. "Never mind, Billy, just a joke."

"Oh, right. Sure. A daughter, huh? That's great." Billy sounded very pleased.

Kyle was beginning to think the boy couldn't put on an act if he wanted to.

"Marcie's okay?" Billy asked.

"Marcie's fine."

"Good, good. Um, can I...can I maybe come see her? At the hospital, I mean."

"I think she'd like that, yes. She's in Maitland Maternity."

"The famous place, right. She told me that's where she'd go." Kyle could hear a restlessness seeping into Billy's voice. "Hey, man, thanks for calling and telling me, you know? I appreciate it. Really."

"No problem."

"But, um, I gotta go. Got a big exam in Chem tomorrow. My dad'll have my head if I don't do well."

Definitely not husband material, not yet, Kyle thought. "I understand perfectly. Goodbye, Billy."

He hung up and shook his head, his hand still on the receiver. Sometimes, he decided, Marcie could see more clearly than he could.

He owed her an apology.

He looked up and down the hall once more. No familiar walk greeted his eyes. If there was nothing wrong, why wasn't Abby coming out to tell him so? And if there was something wrong...if there was something wrong, she should have sent someone out to tell him that, too. If he didn't get some answers soon, he was going to start taking the place apart, brick by brick.

And then he saw her.

Abby was just coming out of a room at the far end of the hall. She glanced around and then found him. The white lab coat she'd donned flapped around her sides as she hurried to him.

Kyle cut the distance between them in two heartbeats. "Well?" he demanded.

She saw the concern etched into his face and let the waspish tone slide. They were all a little edgy right now. "Mother and daughter are doing fine." Her exhaustion was returning. Abby sank her hands into her coat.

"What took so long?"

At least he wasn't barking the questions anymore. "Marcie needed a couple of stitches on her head." There was empathy in her smile. "Poor thing is going to be hurting at both ends for a while."

"But she's okay." He just had to hear it one more

time before he could tuck away his concerns on that
score.

"Right as rain." *God, where did that expression
come from?* She was punchier than she thought. "You
were pretty okay back there, too." She smiled. "First
time I ever saw you calm her down instead of incite
her."

He shrugged. On reflection, it had been a pretty awe-
inspiring experience. "Every so often, I rise to the occasion." Relieved, and then agitated again, he heaved
a sigh.

Abby could have cut the tension around him with a
chainsaw. Now what? "What's on your mind?"

He laughed ruefully, hooking his thumbs on his back
pockets, the way he used to when jeans had been the
uniform of the day instead of three-piece suits. "Am I
that transparent?"

You are to me. But she kept that observation to herself. There was no point in his knowing just how tuned
in she was to him.

"Well, I just told you everything's going to be all
right, and you still have that funny little furrow between
your eyebrows." She feathered her fingertip lightly
across it. "So I just assume that means there's something else bothering you."

"There might be." He studied her closely. "Or not."

A corner of her mouth curved. "Well, that makes
things perfectly clear."

He moved to the side as a nurse passed them. It was
too crowded here for him to say what he wanted to say.
"Would you like to get some coffee?"

Coffee at this point would only keep her up and turn
her into a zombie by morning. "No, but I'd like to get
some air. They tell me there's a fresh supply of it just

outside these doors.'' She was already leading the way to the nearest exit. ''Want to check it out?''

He caught up to her quickly enough and swung the door open, holding it while she walked by him. The night was warm, but Kyle slipped his arm around her anyway, drawing her close to him so that it seemed as if they were the same being with two sets of legs.

And two hearts meant to be one. Or so he hoped.

Curiosity gave Abby no peace. She hated not knowing things. ''So what is the mysterious 'this' you're planning on telling me about?''

He wanted to get this right, but the moment he began, he knew he was going to falter. ''You're a very independent woman...''

Amusement tugged at her mouth. ''Sounds like the beginning of a commercial for health insurance.''

He replayed the words in his mind and was forced to agree. ''Maybe. But not the way you mean. It wouldn't be your health that would be affected, but mine.''

She drew her head away to look at him, but it didn't make anything clearer. ''Now you're really losing me.''

The key word glared at him in tall, neon lights. ''That's just it, I don't want to.''

Abby shook her head. Maybe the miracle of birth had really addled him. ''Don't want to what?''

''I don't want to lose you.''

For a moment, she felt as if she'd been struck dumb. No words formed. And then she said haltingly, ''I wasn't under the impression that you had me. I mean...are we a couple?''

He felt like a man who had his entire future riding on the turn of a card. ''Do you want to be?''

She'd schooled herself to be cautious, even when her heart was racing. ''I asked you first.''

They couldn't both hang back. And he didn't want to. Not anymore. "There comes a time when you're going to have to stop playing it safe, Abby. And risk something."

She turned her face up to his. Afraid to hope. "Like?"

He caressed her cheek. "Like your heart."

Suddenly, her mouth went dry. If this wasn't going where she hoped it was, she knew she was going to have to kill him. "Maybe I work better with an example to follow."

"Okay, then here goes." His voice grew stronger. "I love you, Abby. I know you might think you don't need a man in your life, but I'd like to think that maybe you do, and I'd like to be that man—"

"Are we negotiating?"

He laughed shortly. It still wasn't coming out right. "Kind of sounds like that, doesn't it?"

She nodded.

"Hell, I don't know any other way to do it."

"Speak English, Kyle. I'm very fluent in English. Do what?" she said, hardly aware that she was rising on her toes.

"Propose."

She stared at him, stunned, her feet flat on the ground again. "What?"

"Propose."

Her heart began to beat wildly. She wasn't sure just how she managed to get the words out past it, because it had flown up to her throat. "How about, Will you marry me?"

He laughed, pulling her closer into his arms. "Okay, since you asked. Yes. There, that takes the burden off me."

"Hey, wait a minute, I wasn't—"

"Yes, but you will." Before she could say anything further, Kyle kissed her long and hard, giving her his heart. He kissed her until they were both almost breathless.

"Yeah," Abby sighed against his mouth just before he kissed her again. "I guess I will at that."

Kyle was sure of it.

MAITLAND MATERNITY

continues with

CASSIDY'S KIDS

by

Tara Taylor Quinn

No-nonsense Ellie Maitland had goals. Ellie
Maitland had focus. Ellie was determined to
prove herself the best damn administrator
Maitland Maternity hospital had ever seen.
Until Sloan Cassidy reappeared in her life.
He'd shown up in her office with adorable
eighteen-month-old twin daughters and
threatened to break her heart all over again,
just as he had ten years ago.

Available next month

Here's a preview!

"RODEOS, SLOAN?" Cold, suddenly, Ellie thought of the little she knew about the famous cowboy sport. "It's so dangerous."

"I've been competing most of my life."

"But you trained, then. You haven't trained this time."

He looked away, his foot bobbing up and down slowly beside her knee. "The rodeo is merely a commercialized view of what cowboys do everyday, Ellie," he said. "I've been roping calves all month long. The only difference this time will be the spectators."

"What if you get hurt?" She couldn't keep the fear out of her voice. Nor the fact that she cared. A lot.

"I won't."

"What if you do?"

He was looking at her, intently. She was afraid he was reading between the lines and seeing far, far too much.

"I could get hurt every single day I leave this house to work the ranch, El, or drive my truck, or even take a shower. You can't live life being afraid of getting hurt."

His voice had lowered, gaining a timbre she'd never heard before. Somehow they weren't just talking about the rodeo anymore.

"You can if you've been hurt so bad you wanted to die."

Eyes narrowed, Sloan looked suddenly fierce. "Who ever hurt you that badly?" he asked. "Some guy you met in college?"

Ellie shook her head, praying that the tears that were gathering wouldn't fall.

"It was you." Her words were no more than a whisper, sticking in her throat.

He straightened, stared at her hard. "But..."

"Because you didn't want me." Ellie had no idea why she was humiliating herself this way. She only knew it felt good to finally be able to talk about that time in her life. To get it out. Get it over.

"I wanted you." His voice was so strong, so sure.

And Ellie shook her head. "No, you didn't, Sloan, and lying about it only makes it worse. It's okay, I'm a big girl now. And I learned not to play with fire."

"I wanted you." His voice shook.

Ellie meant to blurt out another denial. Her gaze connected with Sloan's, instead. Stayed there. She pretended she saw things she couldn't possibly be seeing. So that when he slid along the couch, she met him halfway. When he took her into his arms, pulled her up against him, she went willing.

Settling her bottom on his lap, he pushed up against her. "See how much I want you?" he whispered. "How much I've always wanted you?"

Heart beating so fast she could hardly breath, couldn't think at all, Ellie felt his arousal, and was lost. Sloan was holding her, his body nudging hers intimately. It was worth dying for.

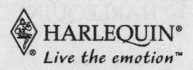

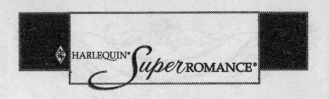
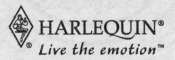

Harlequin Historicals®
Historical Romantic Adventure!

*From rugged lawmen and
valiant knights to defiant heiresses
and spirited frontierswomen,
Harlequin Historicals will
capture your imagination with
their dramatic scope, passion
and adventure.*

*Harlequin Historicals . . .
they're too good to miss!*